BOWMANVILLE

by SIDNEY SHELLEY

BOWMANVILLE BREAK

BREAK

DELACORTE PRESS/NEW YORK

TO JUNE

BOWMANVILLE BREAK

CHAPTER 1

At 8 A.M., a luxuriously late hour for the military, the bugle sounded its melodious notes for morning roll call. Although everyone was presumably awake and at the ready—reveille had been blown a half hour before—not one man emerged from the fieldstone barracks.

Lowering his instrument, the middle-aged corporal-bugler darted a glance at the aging lieutenant standing next to him on the parade grounds of the Bowmanville Prisoner-of-War Camp.

A leftover from World War I, a grandfather assigned to duty in the Veterans' Guard of Canada, the lieutenant snorted in his breath and his girth.

"What the devil!"

He turned to the graying but trim sergeant major.

"Stir them up in there, Sergeant. Get them out on the double," the lieutenant ordered, unwilling to acknowledge the trouble he suspected.

Sergeant Delamare moved resolutely toward Barrack I. It was a damn-fool errand. But it was a face-saver. It was doing it by the book. A spit-and-polish officer couldn't acknowledge rebellion until it showed itself openly. At any rate, the sergeant didn't mind a tough assignment. He was as hard and finely tempered as the double-bitted ax he used to swing. He didn't go about demonstrating it gratuitously, but he had a native understanding of its value in dealing with certain types of beings, human or animal.

Up in the tower commanding that part of the encampment, the guard swiveled the heavy machine gun on its mounting to cover the sergeant and bear on Barrack I. In this war he had never fired a weapon in earnest and he welcomed at least the show of power.

Delamare grasped the door handle and pushed firmly against the door. It didn't budge. There being no lock on the inside, he knew it was wedged. A half hour earlier he himself had led the duty squad which had unbarred the doors of the barracks. They were locked each night after taps but kept open all day.

Delamare's fist thumped on the half timbers of the door. He pretended not to know there was a deliberate reason for the fastening of the door.

"Roll call! Everyone out!"

Silence. The sergeant waited. He never gave an order twice. If the timbre of his voice didn't evoke an immediate response, there was a reason for it that histrionics wouldn't correct.

Inside the barrack, sixty German officers stood stony-faced. Their attention was centered not on the senior officer present, but on Fregattenkapitän Wilhelm Modersohn, who stood apart from the group with his first officer, Leutnant Otto von Sperle, at his side. In the rear of the barrack, as though holding himself aloof from the proceedings, was General Alfred von Westhofen, senior officer in Bowmanville, formerly of the Afrika Korps. Next to him stood his ADC, Kapitän Walther Linke. About eighty per cent of the officers wore the same uniform as Modersohn, the blue of the Kriegsmarine with an Unterseeboot medal on the left breast.

After allowing a thirty-second period of suspense to tick by, Modersohn nodded his head composedly at the general and his aide. Von Westhofen remained immobile. Linke glanced at his superior and, with all eyes following him, marched uneasily to the door.

"Sergeant Delamare," he called. "The general's compliments to Colonel Perry. He will speak only to the colonel."

Staring at the door as though it would answer, the mild-looking little captain waited for an acknowledgement. In Modersohn's otherwise composed face, a pulse in his temple throbbed visibly.

Delamare knew how to play the game, too. He turned from the door without replying, his woodsman's feet making no more noise than the curl of his lip as he strode back to report. On the verge of calling out again, Linke was silenced by a barely perceptible shake of Modersohn's head.

The Fregattenkapitän Modersohn—known behind his back as Silent Willi—was coordinating the action like an orchestra conductor. This was the opening chord of a *marche militaire* which was to take him back to Germany. As thoroughly as he had plotted the attacks which had made him the U-boat ace of Germany, he was plotting this campaign. Modersohn was not going to lapse into obscurity in a POW camp. Not Silent Willi Modersohn. He was going to return to the battle, to fight to the end. To the bitter end—and then some.

CHAPTER 2

At 8 A.M. that same morning of June 14, 1943, in Halifax, Nova Scotia, Captain Robert Gallant, onetime newspaperman, recent combat intelligence officer and presently flotsam of war, was disembarking from a troopship. He wanted nothing more than peace, figuratively and literally. To be left alone and to let alone.

As he set foot on the quay a shore officer saluted and inquired: "Captain Robert Gallant?"

"Don't tell me," he said with a forced grin. "Orders."

The officer handed him an envelope. He tore it open and unfolded the sheet of plain paper it contained.

"No orders," he amended, recognizing the bluff handwriting in soft editing pencil. "Thanks."

He read the note: "Come see me before you do anything. Welcome home. Kerr."

No, Kerr didn't give orders. He gave assignments. Even now that he was a general he was still operating as he had when he was a newspaper editor. It was strictly in the Kerr tradition to find out exactly what ship he was on and to scratch out a succinct message. No army forms in triplicate to yellow away in concert with the archivists who preserve them.

On his arrival in Ottawa, Gallant went round to the Roxborough, where he had maintained an apartment during his days as a newspaper correspondent. He was given a warm welcome and the "last apartment" which is always maintained by hotels for special guests. Across the street were the ugly temporary wooden buildings adjoining the Ministry of National Defense, where he knew Kerr was now ensconced. After a leisurely wash and a change of uniform, Gallant decided to pay his call immediately, more out of a desire to see Kerr once again than in response to his summons.

Kerr was one of the fast-disappearing types of great editors, an individualist to whom the gathering of news was a sport with no holds barred. To the confoundment of the military-establishment types, Kerr had been appointed to the wartime task for which he was uniquely capable. He was a brigadier in charge of a bureau in counterintelligence. Intelligence being largely a matter of the acquisition and coordination of information, Kerr was an expert at organizing it.

Kerr squinted at Gallant through the smoke of the black cigarette which bobbed between his lips and came straight to the point.

"I'm requesting you for my staff, if it's okay with you."

For a moment it seemed to Gallant that it would be okay with him. The atmosphere got to him. The smell of the pungent cigarettes Kerr smoked made the office seem like the old city room. And even the uniform didn't change Kerr. It was sloppy, unpressed, the lapels covered with ashes, which he brushed away ineffectually whenever a live spark seemed too threatening. But it was still the army, Gallant reminded himself, and the only sufferable place in the army was in a battle zone. Otherwise one was the only thing worse than a bureaucrat: a uniformed bureaucrat.

"It's not okay, Kerr. I'm not your man. I wouldn't like it. I'd just mess up the job."

"What will you do then?" Kerr asked. "They're not discharging you even though you are too banged up for overseas duty. They'll have you out on a lecture tour selling bonds or polishing someone's brass in a public relations setup. Your by-line still rings a bell around here and every publicity-seeking SOB in a swivel chair will be requisitioning you. Think you'll like that?"

Gallant ran his fingers through his hair, whose black coloring had seen its first touches of gray only a few months before.

"Kerr, if you want to appeal to my reason, I'll have to admit you are right. But that doesn't change the way I feel. Right now I just want the warrior's reward. I want to lick my wounds in private. I have a leave coming to me and I want to go away and forget."

"Look, boy," Kerr used persuasive, fatherly tones, "don't throw yourself away. Go take your rest and then come back here. You know I wouldn't be in this chair unless I was free to do a decent job without my hands' being tied. And I can't accomplish a damn thing unless I have some men with me who have the sense to know a lead when they see one."

"Okay," Gallant decided abruptly, "you've hired yourself an ex-reporter with an atrophied lung. But I get to take a vacation first. It says so in my papers—three weeks."

"Vacations," Kerr snorted. "They atrophy the brain. You can use my cabin if you like. Just move in. It's all ready. And don't bother replacing the whiskey. I never get up there myself these days."

To Lieutenant Colonel Arthur Perry, commander of the Veterans' Guard at Bowmanville, the order which sparked that day's events was a lamentable error in judgment. Nevertheless, he would execute it. The order in question specified that he was to manacle seventy of the prisoners in his camp in retaliation for the manacling of Canadian prisoners in Germany. In Colonel Perry's opinion, two wrongs did not make a right, a proverb he had often resorted to in his civilian occupation as the principal of a high school. However, as a public servant and a former line officer he understood the immutability of orders. To be sure, there was a certain amount of flexibility in their application, and Colonel Perry had tried to soften the manacling order by advising the senior officer of the prisoners of it the night before. The order was to be carried out that morning.

His porcelain-toned face showing strain, Perry regarded the ordered perfection of each object on his flat-top desk as he listened to Delamare's report on the prisoners' disobedience. He knew the sergeant had disapproved notifying the Germans that they were to be shackled. Having made the blunder, Perry decided to carry the weight on his own shoulders. He adjusted the pince-nez glasses, which narrowed his face.

"Tell General von Westhofen I'll be down to confer with him."

Typical of top sergeants, Delamare made suggestions by inference.

"You mean after roll call, sir?"

Perry held his head very straight, looked directly at the sergeant.

"I'll be down to speak to him directly. That's all, Sergeant," he added.

He waited until Delamare had saluted and left before summoning his adjutant.

"Captain Howell, turn out every available man in battle dress. Hold them outside the compound gate until further orders."

"Why don't you let me go down and speak to them, sir? As a matter of form. Doesn't do to give those Prussians too much importance." Howell spoke with the assurance of his trade. In civilian life he was a gym instructor.

"That's just it, Howell, a little concession from me is all they're looking for. They'll come along quietly enough after that. This is just a token—passive resistance. They had the same sort of trouble in the other camps, you know."

Bowmanville was a day behind the others in complying with the shackling order. Not enough handcuffs were immediately available. At a few of the other camps, Perry had been informed, the prisoners had put up a mild form of passive resistance, the minimum necessary to register their disapproval. Such wasn't Modersohn's intention, as the colonel was to discover shortly.

"We refuse to submit to this violation of the Geneva Convention," Perry was told through the barricaded door of Barrack I by General von Westhofen, repeating the words imposed upon him by his willful junior, Modersohn.

"Your protest is academic," the high-school principal tried to reason. "Your country started this, as you well know from the newspapers which are at your disposal. My government is taking the only means available to it to force discontinuance of this practice."

"Colonel, as a prisoner of war I can only abide by the articles governing such conditions and I cannot accept the propaganda of your newspapers or the ruses of your government. We are prepared to remain barricaded in here until you give us guarantees of immunity from manacling. I officially request you to call Maag, the representative of the Swiss Protecting Power in the Sun-Life Building in Montreal," he added with precision, "and make known our position."

"You leave me no choice but to resort to force, General von Westhofen. Please reconsider. I'll give you fifteen minutes in which to come out."

"Not necessary. We will resist force with force. You'll have to conquer all eight hundred of us before you can shackle seventy."

Von Westhofen turned away from the door and Modersohn gave his next signal. A rich baritone voice started the first notes of the Horst Wessel song. Immediately, the fifty-nine other voices in the barrack joined in. Then, as in singing a round, one barrack after another took up the tune in measured intervals. By the time the colonel rejoined his adjutant outside the compound gates, the anthem had swelled provocatively from all seven of the long stone structures in the prisoners' compound.

Short of using firearms against the prisoners, which he had never contemplated, Perry realized that his force was inadequate to the task. He had one company—a hundred and twenty-five men—of World War I veterans, most of them physically soft, to handle eight hundred active young men in peak condition. Far from suffering from their imprisonment, they had better food and living conditions than in their own services.

A fair tactician, Perry held his main force under Captain Howell inside the gate in the zone forbidden to prisoners. This zone, thirty yards wide, stretched from the wall to a two-foot-high trip wire running all around the compound. Any prisoner crossing the wire was automatically considered an escapee and could be fired upon legitimately.

Hoping to squelch the uprising by depriving it of its leader,

Perry dispatched Sergeant Delamare with a strengthened squad to take Barrack I. Although the guards in the machine-gun towers trained their weapons in support of Delamare, the troops were under strict orders not to fire unless the prisoners attempted to break out of the compound.

As Delamare led his squad away from the gate, the organized singing—now having progressed to "Deutschland über Alles"—stopped. The sudden silence was ominous.

The squad advanced, the men carrying only clubs, a precautionary measure to avoid more sophisticated weapons' falling into the hands of the prisoners. Delamare was familiarly hefting a lumberjack's ax.

Inside the barracks a man was posted at each of the small barred windows. Signals were going back and forth from building to building. In all the barracks, the men were armed with primitive weapons. Most held stout clubs of varied materials. Some swung wicked flails studded with nails and jagged bits of metal. One compact group held a collection of rocks and stones at the ready.

Except for those posted at the windows, the eyes of every man in Barrack I were on the submarine captain. As in a torpedo drill, the man at the window facing the gate sang out the approach of the squad.

"Fifty meters . . . forty meters . . . thirty meters . . ."

No one moved.

"Twenty meters."

Modersohn remained like a statue, instilling his discipline in the others.

"Ten meters."

A man stationed at the door, holding the handle, tightened his muscles.

"Five meters. Two meters."

Those holding stones drew back their arms. Leaping back,

the man at the door threw it open. Delamare, his ax circling, was taking a last few giant strides toward it. Lithely, Delamare dodged to the side. A fast-flying stone rang on the upheld blade of his ax, directly in line with his head. In another bound he reached a sheltered position next to the door.

Confused, some of the squad expected that the opening of the door meant surrender; others were simply not alert enough to follow their sergeant's lead. At deadly range they were caught by the hail of rocks thrown from inside the room. Three men managed to reach the noncom's side, only grazed by the missiles. The rest of the twenty-man squad was heavily pelted. The two leading men, a forty-five-year-old grocer and a forty-eight-year-old stock-market clerk, were knocked unconscious. Several others were badly bruised. The squad retreated, dragging away their wounded. Flattened against the side of the building, Delamare, yelling imprecations, brandished his ax in the open door to discourage pursuit of his fleeing squad. At a signal from within, the barrage ceased.

Borrowing a club from one of the men who had joined him, Delamare contrived to jam open the door.

"Give up now," he ordered. "Throw out your weapons."

Laughter and jeers greeted the proposal.

"Okay then, don't. But don't try to get out," he warned them. "The first man who tries to get out will get this ax through his brain."

"It's all right! We're comfortable where we are! Come get us!" the prisoners shouted.

Following the action from the gate watch tower, Colonel Perry realized that this was not an impromptu demonstration. Organization and planning were apparent here. The preparations must have been made some time in advance. He had given notice of the shackling order only the night before. There hadn't been sufficient time or opportunity since then to collect the stones and the other weapons the prisoners had. Nor had there been time to organize the signal system, the singing, the whole offensive structure. He had no doubt but what the prisoners had stores of food as well. It was customary for prisoners to hoard supplies, usually from Red Cross packages, to be used for escape purposes. No, it had all been prepared in advance and was awaiting only the propitious moment.

Although confronted by superior forces if it came to hand-to-hand fighting, Perry was reluctant to appeal for help against unarmed prisoners. He also felt that he could not await its arrival even if he were willing to sacrifice his pride. Immediate action was necessary. Delamare and his three men were pinned to the barrack wall. The mess-hall squad which began work at six o'clock every morning, was isolated within the compound. And in addition, for psychological reasons, he couldn't allow the prisoners to win even one round.

The main danger, Perry realized, lay not in the small force in Barrack I, but in the reserves in the six as yet unengaged barracks. He could only hope that the prisoners would not dare an outright confrontation, that they would be inhibited by the futility of their gesture.

By the time the stragglers of Delamare's squad reached the gate, Perry had given his orders. Captain Howell was leading half the remaining force in an attack on Barrack I. Strung out in a skirmish line to minimize the effectiveness of another rock barrage, they made for the open door at a ragged trot. The rest of the Veterans, split into two columns, each under a lieutenant, entered the encampment to protect the flanks of the main group from attack by those in the other barracks.

Brandishing his ax in the doorway, Delamare reminded the prisoners of his presence. While he diverted them, one of his men made a flying dash for the opposite side of the door. He waved his club in the doorway, yelling:

"Now try something!"

Modersohn exacted the same discipline he demanded while stalking a convoy. His men remained quiet, awaiting orders. A Panzer leutnant at the front window reported:

"The last man has cleared the trip wire, Kapitän. They're all inside now."

Fifteen seconds passed before Modersohn moved. He pointed an index finger at an officer stationed at a side window. The officer pumped his arm in the air three times. An answering signal came from Barrack II and the alert was thus passed from barrack to barrack.

Moving warily, the Canadian troops came within fifty feet of Barrack I. Suddenly, the din of eight hundred shouting, screaming voices halted them. Pouring out of the other six barracks came the full force of prisoners, all waving clubs, flails or bags of stones.

On orders from their officers, the Canadian troops halted, drew on gas masks. The flanking columns obliqued in toward the skirmishers, who once again continued their advance toward the beleaguered barrack, which resumed its stoning tactics. In reply, Howell, an enthusiastic trout fisherman, used his best casting technique to lob a gas grenade directly into Delamare's cupped hands.

Delamare pulled the pin, counted ten and then another two for good measure. With a circular swing, he sent the grenade sizzling into the room, hitting one of the closely bunched officers squarely in the chest, knocking him breathless. Tear gas billowed throughout the room. Momentary confusion reigned as those nearest the grenade scurried, stumbled back. Modersohn's sharp voice restored order.

"Breathe through your handkerchiefs." He pulled his out as an example. "Your handkerchiefs . . . use them.

"Now then, the men with stones, prepare to give me a volley through the door, then everyone rush it."

Forewarned by the gas masks, the majority of the prisoners sprinted toward the Canadian lines in an effort to reach them before the grenades could be thrown. As soon as they were within range, those carrying stones loosed their missiles with effective results. A number of Canadians dropped or doubled over in pain.

At almost the same time, the Canadian lieutenants, judging the rioters near enough and closely enough bunched, sang out orders for grenades to be launched. Some few of the attackers had already reached the troopers and were exchanging blows with them. Temporarily outnumbered, the POWs nevertheless gave more than they received, the Canadians being hampered by their masks as well as by their age.

The second wave of rioters, caught by the exploding grenades, was impeded but not stopped outright. Diluted by the fresh air and dispersed by the wind, the tear gas had a minimal effect. Only slightly weakened, the prisoners closed with the soldiers and were still able to swarm over the numerically inferior force.

Seeing the situation, Delamare realized Barrack I could not be taken and decided to put its forces out of action by penning them in. At the same instant Modersohn shouted the order: "Now!"

A lethal volley of stones swept through the doorway. Despite it, Delamare exposed himself to rip away the baton he had wedged between the door and the jamb. Numbing blows struck his left arm as he did so. Reaching around with his right arm, he gripped the heavy crosspiece in the center of the door and, the thick nails of his blunted fingers digging into the rough log, he swung the door shut in the face of a frantic lunge by the prisoner nearest it. The outside bolt was shot home by the soldier standing next to him.

All the more desperate for their tears and coughing, the men inside ineffectually threw their weight against the door. His eyes streaming, Modersohn withdrew the handkerchief from his face to give orders that the heavy refectory table in the center of the room be used as a battering ram.

With Barrack I out of action, Howell saw that he was free to throw the support of his skirmishers to the flanking guardsmen. It was a whirling, striking mass into which they rushed. Howell loosed a few more grenades with more telling effect than the previous ones. A number of Canadians whose long-snouted masks had been torn from their faces fell victim to the gas as well as many of the prisoners.

The Canadians formed a cohesive body. Gasping POWs stumbled away from the melee. Those remaining fought with less force and enthusiasm. The guardsmen hammered their way toward the gate, carrying or supporting their wounded. At the trip wire the fighting ceased, the prisoners either fearful of that boundary beyond which there was open season on them or having received orders to respect that line.

When the last of his men had emerged from the compound, the gate securely locked behind them and the wounded packed off to the infirmary, Colonel Perry had a message broadcast to the prisoners. Captain Howell's voice came over the camp public-address system instructing all wounded prisoners to line up opposite the gate for escort to the dispensary. It was a useless appeal.

As though oblivious to the offer, the POWs milled around the grounds, talking in small groups. The more seriously wounded had been taken inside Barrack II, located directly in front of the gate to the compound. Others, visibly suffering slight injuries, limped about. All the men from Barrack I, having been released by their comrades as soon as the Canadians withdrew, were lying outdoors in the sun, drawing cooling breaths of pine-scented air into their heaving lungs. But not one man lined up for medical treatment by the camp surgeon. Modersohn had decreed that there would be no contact or communication with the camp authorities until the shackling issue was resolved. The two doctors among the prisoners were making do with the medication hoarded against this emergency.

Considering the number of men involved, there were few serious injuries. Two POWs had suffered broken forearms, there were three cases of concussion and multiple bruises and minor cuts. The most painful injury was sustained by the officer who had received the full burning blast of the gas grenade.

Among the Canadians, helmet liners had averted head injuries but one private had four broken ribs, another had his wrist fractured. No count was taken of those treated for contusions and cuts.

With his forces depleted and the prisoners demonstrating their intention of continuing resistance, Colonel Perry decided to try a second, personal appeal before summoning reinforcements. Now that it had been lost, the saving of face took on more realistic proportions and seemed hardly to count. The prisoners had won the first round, there was no getting away from that. They were in control of the compound and he had failed to rescue the marooned mess-hall team. But, theoretically at least, they were not in danger. The mess hall, like the recreation hall, was protected by strong steel shutters over the doors and windows. Unless the prisoners had obtained some unusual tools, they could not force them.

In letter-perfect although accented German, the camp commander gave his ultimatum over the loudspeaker.

"This is Colonel Perry speaking. I wish to make an appeal to reason. I request all prisoners to report for roll call and desist from any further disobedience to regulations. If there is not immediate compliance, I shall have to resort to the use of force. The result will be further bloodshed and withdrawal of all special privileges. You can gain nothing by this demonstration.

This is your last chance. Form ranks immediately for roll call."

Not a man gave indication of having heard, much less of obeying, the colonel's appeal to reason.

There was only one pair of ears which might have heard it with sympathy. They belonged to Luftwaffe Leutnant Günther Schröder, who at that moment was standing at attention before von Sperle, acting in the capacity of disciplinary officer.

Von Sperle was seated at the center of the refectory table. Two officers flanked Schröder. Modersohn stood several feet away from von Sperle like a grand inquisitor. Schröder was the only inmate of Bowmanville who had cared—or more likely dared—to ignore Silent Willy's edict.

"Schröder," von Sperle announced in courtroom manner, "you deliberately failed to obey your commander's order and participate in the demonstration this morning. Do you have any defense?"

Schröder ignored von Sperle and addressed himself to the tall, gangling figure of the U-boat captain, a figure the latter liked to think of as aristocratic.

"I am following the rules established for prisoners of war," the young flyer glared defiantly. "You have no right to order me to revolt against the camp authorities."

Hard-eyed, contemptuous, Modersohn considered this brash officer from a rival service. Von Sperle continued like a ventriloquist's dummy.

"Your previous record and attitude have been the object of study already. This episode confirms our doubts about you. Your case shall be dealt with in good time. Dismissed."

Under quarters arrest, Schröder was marched back to his bunk by his brother officers. Modersohn, preempting the authority of the Ältestenrat, the council of elders which semiofficially ruled the prisoners, passed sentence in the absence of the accused.

"You know what to do," he told von Sperle. "A bad weed. They spread if left unchecked. Later, during the fighting— you'll have a good opportunity."

After their noon meal, an ample one composed of hoarded food, Modersohn briefed the leaders of his small army on the battle tactics to be followed. Each barrack had its own commander and was organized as a separate fighting unit, capable of sustaining itself.

A holiday atmosphere, approved by Modersohn as being good for morale, pervaded the camp. Although still prisoners fenced in by walls, barbed wire and machine guns, there was a feeling of liberty—or rather independence. Inside their little universe, they were the masters.

In midafternoon a convoy of trucks arrived in Bowmanville with the reinforcements Colonel Perry had urgently requested. A company of military police trained in handling mobs and recalcitrant soldiers poured out of the personnel carriers and formed up in perfect drill. Their captain, a former police sergeant, passed them in critical review, then dismissed them with orders to wait on the spot.

Briefed by Colonel Perry, Captain Bannoch turned down the suggestion of a joint operation.

"My men are used to handling this sort of situation," he told the colonel. "They'll operate better on their own without having to worry about troops who are green to these things."

And to his company he said:

"Okay, men, you're lucky. You don't have to wait till you're overseas to get in your licks at these bastards. Now we're under orders to coddle these boys," he winked, "so don't rough them up any more than you have to.

"And remember, when we get in there, stick together. There are more of them than there are of us so I don't want anyone getting off on his own where they can gang up on you. Okay now, let's go."

White truncheons swinging, gleaming in the June sun, the MPs marched through the gate in a column of two. In the forbidden zone inside the trip wire, Bannoch halted the company and reformed it in a skirmish line. Taking the lead in the center of the line, he waved his truncheon above his head, then swung it forward. He moved out toward the few hundred watchful POWs who were assembled in groups of four to six in front of the three barracks facing the parade ground immediately opposite the gate.

The rest of the prisoners—some six hundred who were housed in the four larger barracks to the rear—were nowhere in evidence. If Bannoch was troubled by this, he gave no sign of it. Stepping over the trip wire, he led his men at an unfaltering pace toward the unmilitary-looking enemy formation ninety yards away.

As the MPs came into throwing range, Bannoch ordered them forward in a charge he hoped would upset the aim of the Germans as well as bring them to grips faster. The aim of the Germans was indeed not so accurate as it would have been against slower targets. Some of the MPs were hit, several rendered *hors de combat*, but the others swept on to where they could bring their truncheons into play.

The POWs, except for the few saber devotees among them, fared poorly and fell back as the weighted truncheons battered against their improvised clubs.

Pressing their advantage, the MPs were not prepared for Modersohn's counterattack. Observers in the watch towers stood helpless to give warning as the men in the four large barracks emerged, unseen by the MPs, and slipped silently around to attack them from the rear.

Their first onslaught caused high casualties among the sur-

with cold steel—bayonets. A solid line of bayonets coming toward them will set their tripes in an uproar."

"No bloodshed," Perry insisted worriedly. "I don't want men being cut up or gutted in there."

"We won't have to use them," Bannoch promised. "Bayonets are psychological weapons. They'll put their tails between their legs when they see them. Anyway, I'll give the men orders to club their rifles if it comes to trouble. But I'm sure it won't."

Reluctantly, Perry yielded.

Precisely as the sun showed on the horizon, Bannoch marched his mixed bag of MPs and Veterans' Guard through the gate, their bayonets fixed and gas masks at the ready. It was a still, clear morning.

Even before the steel-barred gates were opened, however, sentries on the inside gave the warning. Already up and about, the Germans were not taken by surprise. Disheveled, unshaven, the prisoners awaited them, not so frolicsome as on the previous day, their tempers at the quick, suffering in the early dawn from a cold breakfast and the lack of the creature comfort of a good wash.

Thrown with a vengeance, a volley of stones opened the second day of battle. But no German stood his ground to meet Bannoch's cold steel. Nor was he able to herd them into groups so that tear gas would be effective. Dancing, jeering, they retreated. The Canadians pursued them clumsily, burdened with their rifles, gas masks, military impediments. The grounds were too vast, their numbers too small, to corner the prisoners. Picking up the stones used against them, the Canadians returned the missiles, their sole recourse. After a few hours, with minor casualties on both sides, Bannoch led his winded men out.

That afternoon, yielding to an inspiration of Colonel Perry, he accepted civilian aid. News of the POW revolt had been carefully kept from leaking out of the camp, not only on the

prised soldiers at either end of the Canadian line. In the center, locked in hand-to-hand combat like the others, Bannoch had lost the reins of command although the bull-like MP captain was clearing his immediate vicinity of all opposition.

At the same time as the German reinforcements left their barracks, Günther Schröder was herded out onto the field of battle.

"This time you're joining us," he was told by one of the two officers assigned to watch him. Pushed out of the door, shoved along, he tried to make sense of this unexpected conscription. A ringing blow on the side of the head answered his attempt to hold back. Stunned, one officer holding him under each arm, Schröder was dragged to the fray.

"Maybe some Canadian will take care of him for us," he heard one of his escorts snigger.

A shove sent him reeling into the truncheon of an MP. A glancing blow caught him on the shoulder, knocking him to one side. Out of the corner of his eye he saw a club descending on him, wielded by one of his escorts. Schröder tried to fling himself out of the way. Another glancing blow. The fellow officer who directed it was hit by an MP. Schröder managed to get his feet under him and start running.

A guard in the machine gun tower noticed a prisoner running in the open, midway between the swirling, battling mass and the trip wire. A second German officer appeared, apparently pursuing him. He gained ground rapidly, finally bringing him to earth with a flying tackle. The two men grappled furiously on the ground. Finally, the first one caught the other's throat in the crook of his arm and held him in a choking grasp. Despite frenzied blows, he held fast till the second officer collapsed. Then he got up, staggered toward the trip wire, fumbled in his pocket and pulled out a white handkerchief, which he waved.

Mistrustful though he was after that day's demonstrations, the soldier behind the machine gun aimed at Schröder was not trigger happy. Fortunately so, for as Schröder reached the trip wire he saw the gates swing open and he rushed forward into the forbidden zone, interpreting the opening as a response to his signal.

The gates were opening to permit the passage of all the able-bodied members of the Veterans' Guard company that Colonel Perry could muster. Despite Bannoch's earlier refusal, he was sending in reinforcements. They parted to let the dazed Luftwaffe officer through their ranks as they dogtrotted to the fray for the second time that day. The colonel himself took charge of Schröder.

"They tried to murder me!" the POW gasped.

"Nonsense," the colonel protested. "We're only trying to enforce regulations."

"No, you don't understand. Not your men. My own people—they want to murder me."

Busy rounding up his reinforcements, Perry hadn't seen the incident between the two officers. He took in the bedraggled condition of the leutnant and concluded that it was a touch of hysteria touched off by a fairly savage beating.

"Get this man to the dispensary," he ordered a medical corpsman standing by.

"But . . . ," Schröder tried to continue. The corpsman led him away. Perry was too preoccupied to listen to the ravings of a shock case. His men had just reached the battle line.

Profiting from his previous experience, Howell kept his men in a compact group rather than spread them thin against the overwhelming enemy force. Driving through the center of the fighting, Howell connected up with Bannoch, whose towering form he could make out from afar.

With the help of the fresh troops, Bannoch managed to rally

his command, his voice ringing out: "To me! To best tradition of the old-time military adventure which he was addicted. Forming a defense dating Roman legions—the hollow square—the combine forces gradually managed to push their way back to sanctuary of the two-foot-high wire barrier.

Each side withdrew to care for its wounded and of evening drew an uneasy lull over Bowmanville. were high in terms of minor injuries: fractures and c cuts and bruises. In terms of the war which was be cuted, they were a bagatelle.

Morale ran high among the prisoners despite thei or perhaps because of them. Almost every man boaste a black-and-blue mark to prove his contribution to the

In the dusk, campfires illuminated groups of pri they set about preparing their evening meal. Their foo was still adequate although they had only a limited a water, stored by order of their farseeing chief in eve able container. Perry had had both the water and the el cut inside the compound.

Furious but chastened, Bannoch conferred with Pe agreed to defer further action till the following mornin time he accepted the cooperation of the Bowmanville n was adamant in refusing to request more troops from o Pride and the thought of how it would look on his reco cluded this altogether.

"Give me an alternative then," Perry countered. "It's o we can't control them with the forces we have."

"I used kid gloves today," the big captain argued. "T row it'll be another story. We'll hit them early before th prepared. If there's no breeze we'll give them a taste o again. Really saturate the area. If we can't use gas, we'll

usual basis of secrecy with which the military frequently cloaks its errors, but also to avoid alarming the neighboring civilian population. However, local police units had been warned and through them Perry arranged to requisition some equipment from the Bowmanville fire department.

When the gates were opened for the afternoon session, the POWs faced three pumpers equipped with six high-pressure hoses. Disabling streams of water tumbled the men who dared linger within striking distance. Some few were seized and made prisoner for a second time. Most of the eight hundred Germans retreated to distant parts of the compound, beyond the mess and recreation halls, where the tennis courts and playing field were located. In doing so they lost their barracks and with them their reserve supplies.

Small squads of the Veterans' Guard were installed in each barrack; they barricaded the doors and windows so they could not be retaken. The cook and his assistants in the mess hall were relieved of their not too disagreeable sojourn in the well-stocked mess hall and nine wounded prisoners together with their two medical officers were taken from Barrack II to the infirmary.

It was a victory for the Canadians but still a stalemate. Dusk that second evening found them holding on to the positions they had gained. They stayed within the compound. Their high-pressure hoses held the Germans at the far end, but they were still unsubmissive. Supperless, some of them in damp clothing, showing little enthusiasm for the continued rebellion, the prisoners were held in line by the determination of their purposeful leader.

By holding out as long as possible, Modersohn had an objective in mind other than the trifling expenditure of Canadian manpower and resources. He hoped to embarrass both Colonel Perry *vis-à-vis* his superiors, and the Allies in their relations with the Swiss, the protecting power for the German POWs.

An embarrassed camp commander can be useful. Having had one incident in his command—and perhaps a reprimand for it—he is anxious to avoid another and may be prone to leniency. That is, if he is not driven the other way and made to be a martinet. However, Modersohn's accurate appraisal of Perry's character allowed him to discount the latter possibility. In fact, he considered the main risk to be the replacement of Perry, a reasonable officer, by a more strict type. It was a risk to be run and his intelligence sources informed him that Perry's reputation was sufficiently good to withstand a minor black mark.

On the third morning of the strike, Perry was awake before dawn had properly lightened the sky. In the bathroom of his two-room apartment in the officers' quarters, he was trying to brush the bad taste of anxiety from his mouth. A knock on the door was a welcome interruption to his thoughts about the impending day. In a late-evening conference, Bannoch had proposed draconian measures against the now herded prisoners. It could mean bloodshed if they refused to surrender. Perry had been forced to accept.

"Come in!" Perry yelled from the bathroom, hastily wiping remnants of toothpaste from the corners of his mouth, looking most unmilitary in an old checked flannel bathrobe.

Equally disheveled and red-eyed, Lieutenant Eldridge, who was the night duty officer, came into the living room waving a sheet of paper.

"Saved by the bell, Arthur." He handed the paper to Perry, his next-door neighbor and friend of twenty years' standing, with whom he had discussed Bannoch's plan the night before.

"No more manacling. Message just came in on the teletype. The Nazis called it quits."

Perry rapidly scanned the paper to confirm in black and white Eldridge's news.

"Thanks, Dave. Would you mind telling Howell and Bannoch to meet me in my office in ten—better make it fifteen—

minutes. They might not be up yet. And then get the interpreter on the PA system and ask General von Westhofen to confer with me in a half hour. Escort him up yourself, will you?"

"Have some breakfast with me first, Arthur. You look like you need it. Bit green around the gills for a CO."

"After, Dave. Between us, I don't think I could get it down yet. How are things out there this morning?"

Eldridge unself-consciously waved a hand which had three fingers missing—a barely remembered sacrifice to the charnel house of World War I.

"All quiet. Nothing's changed since last night."

"Achtung! Achtung!" the loudspeaker rang in German. The use of that language was mainly courtesy. The majority of the German officers spoke English, some extremely well. All those who didn't were taking courses in the language on the express orders of their commander.

"A message for General von Westhofen, please," the interpreter continued. "Colonel Perry requests General von Westhofen to confer with him in his office in thirty minutes."

Modersohn crossed the grounds to the spot where von Westhofen had bedded down.

"I'll accompany you."

"Naturally," von Westhofen answered drily. His tone indicated nothing, neither acceptance or rejection.

Clothes freshly brushed by their orderlies, clean-shaven thanks to a kit carried by the general's man, von Westhofen, his ADC and Modersohn marched from the far side of the camp at precisely the appointed hour, passed the Canadian MPs manning the firefighting equipment and came to a halt at the trip wire in front of the gate.

Eldridge advanced from the gate to meet them.

"My aides will accompany me, Lieutenant," the general dictated.

"Very well, General." There was nothing in the books against it and Eldridge knew Perry well enough to be sure he would overlook the general's assumption of privilege.

When Perry acquainted the trio with the news, he remarked: "This would seem to resolve our differences, gentlemen. I suggest you order your subordinates to resume the normal camp routine. You realize, of course, that I am obliged to exact certain punishment."

Von Westhofen raised a questioning eyebrow and at the same time nodded his head. Impossible to tell if he was assenting or dissenting. Modersohn's gray eyes narrowed as though to see the problem more clearly.

"I don't know if we can agree under such circumstances," von Westhofen took his cue.

Perry's patience found its end.

"There are rules governing this situation. If you do not choose to comply, I shall order Captain Bannoch to use whatever measures are necessary to enforce them."

There was no mistaking Perry's determination. His flat tones, grim features, spoke plainly. Modersohn knew he had gone to the limit of his possibilities. It was time to conciliate.

"With the general's permission," he half bowed to von Westhofen. "What punishment does the colonel propose?"

"The details will be read to you at roll call this evening," the colonel said severely. "However, I will tell you now that payment for all repairs to damaged property will be deducted from the prisoners' pay and there will be certain losses of privileges for a limited time."

Bowing his head, Modersohn acquiesced silently. He realized Perry's sentence could have been much heavier. Solitary confinement, the heaviest burden for a prisoner's morale, would not have been out of order.

"Very well, Colonel," von Westhofen consented.

"You may keep my full salary," Modersohn offered, "if you will deduct less from the other men."

"The lower ranks bear as much guilt for following as the upper echelons do for leading, and it's time they learned that lesson," Perry retorted.

"I might add, General von Westhofen, that as senior officer of the prisoners, in accordance with custom you were allowed to represent your comrades. I feel you have violated your trust and destroyed the harmony of our working relationship. Your value as spokesman for the prisoners is severely impaired in my eyes. For the moment, you will restrict your functions to passing on my orders."

Modersohn eyed the two men gravely. Von Westhofen stood up, clicked his heels and said: "By your leave." He turned and strode to the door, Linke following.

"That is all," Perry dismissed Modersohn as well.

CHAPTER 3 "Schröder, get your things!" the medical orderly sang out from the door of the ward. "You're going back this afternoon. You too, Fahrenburg!" He indicated the only other patient in the ward, a U-boat leutnant who had been among those captured when they were bowled over by the water jets. "Nothing more wrong with you. Got a lot of new customers on the way in. We need the beds."

"Corporal," Schröder protested, "there must be some mistake. I'm supposed to stay here. The colonel knows all about it."

"Doctor's orders," the wizened orderly shrugged. "It's for your boys, not ours. Some of them got banged up pretty good in the fighting, too. They're bringing them over now."

Reluctant to speak freely in front of Fahrenburg, Schröder got up from the bed where he had been reading and approached the orderly.

"I must see the doctor. There's been a mistake. It's dangerous for me to go back. He can't send me back."

"Can and did, Lieutenant. I'm following orders. If you don't like it, you can go through channels just like anyone else. Nothing I can do about it."

To preclude further discussion the corporal slammed the door shut, snapping the bolt in place.

"You'll face the music now," the U-boat leutnant sneered. "Thought they would take care of you, huh?"

Schröder walked over to Fahrenburg menacingly.

"Shut up or there'll be one pig-boat sailor less in the world."

"Traitor."

"Get on your feet and let's see how you fight when you're alone."

The U-boater limited his reply to another sneer. Schröder grabbed the flannel shirting of his pajamas and pulled him to a sitting position.

"Get out of bed and fight for your Greater Germany. They'll give you a brown shirt to go with the brown nose you've got from making up to your kapitän."

Fahrenburg had been a junior officer in Modersohn's U-125.

"I'll report what you're saying."

"Report." Schröder heaved the leutnant out of bed. "Report on your mother, too."

The leutnant tried to push him away. Releasing his hold, Schröder lashed out at him with both fists, sending him crashing into a metal cabinet, which toppled resoundingly.

Diving at Schröder's feet, the U-boat officer brought him to the floor, pushing one wheeled hospital bed into another in the process. The sound of their grappling brought two orderlies into the ward. They tried to separate the two men.

"Here, break that up."

"Can't you Nazis ever stop fighting? Enough of that."

More furniture was overturned, a sheet ripped before the orderlies managed to separate the pair.

"Look at that now." Their wardman contemplated the damage ruefully. "I'll have you up before the doctor for this. Come along! Right now!"

Pushing the two leutnants in front of them, the orderlies herded them to the MO's office, where a flustered doctor tried to act the role of an army disciplinarian.

"What do you mean by fighting in a hospital? Destroying equipment! Who started this?"

"He did, sir," Fahrenburg was quick to reply. "I was just defending myself."

Schröder preferred not to confess to the doctor that he had started the fight deliberately in order to have an opportunity to explain his position to a Canadian officer before being returned to the barracks.

"If you please, sir, I was provoked," he explained. "If you will permit, I'll explain to Colonel Perry. He knows all about it."

"This is my hospital, Lieutenant. You'll explain to me."

"Yes sir." Schröder's back straightened. "It was a controversy about my going back to the barrack. I refused to take part in the revolt the other day and was court-martialed. A kangaroo court. I think I was sentenced to death. I managed to get away during the fighting and surrender to Colonel Perry. That's why I can't go back to the barrack, sir. I must see the colonel."

"If you are pulling my leg, Lieutenant, it'll go hard with you."

"I assure you, sir . . ."

The MO addressed the U-boat leutnant.

"What's your version of this?"

"He is lying, sir," the leutnant said. "He is looking for a way out of the responsibility for the fight."

"Really." The MO looked down his nose at Fahrenburg as at someone who was not playing by the rules. And to Schröder he said: "I'll speak to the colonel about you. Meanwhile, you may wait in the ward."

As the prisoners filed out of his office the doctor couldn't resist calling out: "Mr. Fahrenburg!" The U-boat leutnant turned.

"I've heard there is a code among officers: that they don't inform on one another."

His face set in puerile obstinacy, Fahrenburg replied: "He is a disgrace to the German officers' corps, that one. A bad German."

Interesting, thought the doctor. *A bad German. A bad Nazi he means. Maybe this is the good German we've all been hoping to discover. If he is sincere, he's too rare a bird to turn back into the cage with the others.*

The medical orderly stuck his head in the door, interrupting the doctor's thoughts.

"They're bringing in the injured men now, sir."

"Get them settled down. I'll be in to see them shortly," he answered, picking up the phone and asking for Colonel Perry.

"Colonel? Dr. Farnsworth here. I've got an interesting case, nonmedically speaking. I think you know something about it already. Chap by the name of Schröder."

He listened for a moment, frowning.

"No, Colonel, I think his story warrants looking into. He could very well be telling the truth, you know. I don't see what he would hope to accomplish otherwise. No, I'm not giving you a professional opinion. I'm not a psychologist and, even if I were, I doubt if I could tell you anything on the basis of a two-minute interview. I'm giving you a commonsense opinion."

"All right, Doctor," Perry conceded, "but I haven't the time to see him immediately and I don't want to take any risks. I'll send someone around for him and have him locked up in the guardhouse. Not that I mean to imply any criticism—but the dispensary seems to be a favorite jumping-off ground for escapers."

Largely because of an innate respect for the professional status of a doctor, Perry made time in his disrupted schedule to interview Schröder that afternoon. The young aviator who sat stiff and correct in the chair opposite his desk seemed the image of the popular concept of a junior German officer: close-cropped blond hair, features regular to the point of nullifying individuality, the sharp eyes, light blue, of a fighter pilot and a body which looked as though it had been trimmed to fit into the cockpit of a pursuit plane.

"Feeling fit again, Lieutenant?" Perry asked.

"Yes, sir. Thank you." He responded rigidly.

"Do you still think your comrades intend to murder you?"

"They've had no reason to change their plans, Colonel, if that's what you mean. And I assure you I am not suffering from delusions of persecution."

"Yes, yes, of course." Perry looked pained at the forthright mention of a mental aberration. "But why would they want to murder you?"

"Because I refused to participate in the uprising. And they've had suspicions about me for some time now, anyway. They suspect that I crashed my plane deliberately so that I could surrender."

"If they thought that, why did they wait all this time to do something about it? You've been a prisoner for over two years."

"The accusation came from a member of my squadron who arrived here recently. I denied it. It was his word against mine and so they didn't do anything about it, but when this revolt began and I wouldn't cooperate, it was my death sentence."

"Was the accusation true?"

"If I say yes, will you believe me?"

"I may," the colonel answered sincerely. "Except that I do find it difficult to believe they were trying to murder you. And even if they were, they certainly wouldn't continue with their plans now that they know you've had an opportunity to reveal them to me."

"It would look like an accident, Colonel. You couldn't prove anything. I've seen it happen in a camp I was in in England. I could tell you about it, but what could you do? What can you do now when I tell you I have been court-martialed here in your own camp where prisoners have no right to hold court?"

The colonel studied his palm, lifted his eyes to meet the leutnant's. Like the MO, he wanted to believe him, wanted to find among his charges one who was not cut out of the same cloth as the others.

"What made you crash your plane? Did you become an anti-Nazi overnight? Pilots are the elite everywhere. You wouldn't have been accepted as one if they felt you weren't to be trusted."

"It didn't happen overnight, Colonel." Schröder searched for a means to explain an evolution about which he himself was not too clear. "I guess there was a seed in me that grew. It was something maybe they overlooked—didn't manage to stamp out. Even I'm not sure I knew it was there all along. When I discovered it, I still had to build up the courage to act. Or maybe I'm wrong about that. It's easy to confuse the two. I deserted . . . when things became rough . . . when I ran the risk of being shot down and killed—killed for something I didn't believe in. Did it take courage to desert . . . or fear?"

Schröder paused, trying to find the answer to the question.

"That seed," Perry queried, "where did it come from? Why haven't the others got it?"

"The seed?" Schröder reflected. "Well, there were Germans against Hitler at the beginning. Then . . . you must know what happened. The concentration camps. Most of them died there. A few came out. But for the most part, those who did weren't against anything any more by the time they were released. My father was one of them. I was very young but I remember. He wasn't the same. He worked and ate and slept . . . and never spoke.

"I . . . I followed along, did the same as all the other boys in my class. I joined the Hitler Youth. And I shouted louder than the others, I think, because I knew I had to atone. That's how I got into the luftwaffe. My squad leader recommended me. He mistook atonement for enthusiasm . . . and maybe it did turn into enthusiasm with habit."

Perry thought of all the little mimics, conformists who had studied under his wing. Schröder's childhood reaction was quite plausible. But his adult deviation was rare. Schröder might turn out to be a fraud, but he had to be given the benefit of the doubt. On humanitarian grounds. Then, too, if Schröder wanted to cooperate, he might prove of value to the intelligence service.

There was some danger, Perry feared, that he was being played for a fool by Schröder. He might be planning an escape which depended on his being transferred or he might be seeking to cause the Canadian authorities some devious embarrassment. There was only one way to find out.

"I'll send a report on you to Ottawa," he promised. "Meanwhile, you can stay on in the guardhouse. It may not be very pleasant being confined to a cell, but you'll be safe there."

Colonel Perry's report, a precise, almost word-for-word account of his discussion with Schröder and of the eyewitness testimony of his flight from the compound, was buck-slipped through counterintelligence in Ottawa four days later. It was among an eight-inch-high pile of papers in the "In" basket on the desk of Brigadier Donald Kerr when he arrived at his office early that morning. With a bloodshot but practiced eye, Kerr sorted rapidly through the pile, casting aside the chaff after the most fleeting of glances. The Bowmanville report caught his attention and he read it through thoroughly. This Colonel Perry might write with the dryness of chalk on a blackboard, he thought, but at least he could recognize a possibility more subtle than a 75-mm. shell. More than one could say for most of the regular army officers.

The brigadier wrote "Gallant" in heavy lead-pencil across the top of the first page and reached for the phone.

In Kerr's lakeside cabin thirty-five miles from Ottawa, Gallant was still abed when the telephone rang.

"Hello, Kerr," he answered, his absentee host being one of the two persons who knew where to reach him. The imprint of the other's head still freshly marked the pillow next to his and he could see her from the window, poised on the dock, ready to plunge in for her morning swim.

"Gallant," Kerr's early-morning croak came through the ear piece, "sorry to disturb you . . ."

"Well then, don't. I'll go back to sleep and we'll pretend you never called. It can only mean bad news with that apologetic beginning."

Kerr ignored his badinage.

"I wouldn't ask you this if I had anyone else on tap capable of doing the job: Can you pull yourself together and get down here?"

"Hell, Kerr, I just got up here. I still have almost three weeks coming to me, remember? The second front isn't going to collapse because I'm not on the spot, is it?"

"I'll make it up to you later, Bob," Kerr wheedled. "This may be a delicate job and I really don't have anyone who can do it."

"Okay, okay. I don't know why a war should change things. I haven't had a real vacation out of you in ten years. Will tomorrow morning be too late? I have a guest here with me."

"Right." Kerr gave his habitual sign off. "First thing in the morning, though."

Kerr's small, sharp eyes noted every detail in Gallant as he settled his tall, bony frame in the leather armchair opposite his desk. Gallant's normally deep-set gray eyes and hollow cheeks had lost the sunken look he had observed at their last meeting. The few days' rest had been sufficient to restore him as far as one could judge by external appearances.

Satisfied, Kerr tossed a sheaf of papers across the desk.

"Here," he grunted.

Gallant scanned the report on Schröder with practiced rapidity.

"Interesting, if true," he commented. "But you didn't call me in here just for this, I presume. It's more in the line of the psychological-warfare boys in Washington. They'd grab him for one of their shortwave broadcasts."

"I know they would," Kerr answered, "but before we get around to that, I want to see what's behind the story. There may be more to it than is apparent. That's why I don't want to put one of those do-it-by-the-number types on it. Can't even get a good cub reporter any more. They send them to officers' school first. That's the army's equivalent of a journalism school. Squares up their heads along with their shoulders."

Gallant laughed. Kerr was a diehard when it concerned the newspaper business. He'd heard him rant about college journalists before.

"Here's the rest of the story." Kerr handed him a folder containing the reports on the three-day riot at Bowmanville. "Digest this and then we'll take it from there."

Gallant got up to leave.

"No, no, just stay where you are and read it."

Gallant gave the army reports a quick rundown and looked up at the brigadier, who was slashing his way through some paper work, attacking it with his copy pencil like a sword.

"Anytime you're ready."

"Right." Kerr flourished his pencil across the document on his desk, marking it with a big "O.K."

"Well, that's the background," Kerr began. "Now I'll fill you in on the rest. Bowmanville is the only POW camp where we've had any real trouble about this shackling business. On top of that came the Schröder affair. There may or may not be a direct connection, but at any rate the two actions seem to indicate definite organization. The riot was certainly extremely well organized. Logically, if there is an organized group, we can assume there must be other things brewing. Usually that goes hand in glove with outside contacts as well—fifth-column sort of thing, Nazi sympathizers, even actual foreign agents. Which explains why we are in on the deal.

"Now." He paused to light a cigarette from the stub of one he had just finished. "I'd like you to go down there and sniff around for a while. Speak to Schröder, see what angles you can find, you know the sort of thing."

Gallant knew very well. He'd been broken in as a legman by Kerr.

"Is there any further background material available?" he queried. "Anything like a morgue in your setup here?"

"We have files of a sort, but they're not well organized. No cross reference, sometimes no simple reference cards. And we certainly don't have a librarian smart enough to know where to put her hands on the relevant material. They go by the alphabet here. You get what you ask for—if it's listed and if it happens to be filed under the classification you specify."

Kerr looked down at his watch. Noon.

"I'd like you to be down at Bowmanville first thing tomorrow morning. No time for you to dig through the files yourself. Let's have some lunch sent in here—the canteen's no worse than you were getting in North Africa—and that'll allow me a free spell to give you the background myself."

Among Kerr's talents, as Gallant knew, his most spectacular was an elephantine memory. He had almost total recall. In the newspaper business, his stunt of taking over the writing of late-breaking stories was spectacular. Without referring to notes or library clips, he would turn out accurate, clean copy, his pudgy fingers flying over a typewriter keyboard with never a break, always in time to beat the deadline.

"You'd know most of what I can tell you," Kerr said modestly, "if you'd been around here longer."

He pushed a buzzer on his desk. "Lunch, Miss Griffon," he ordered when a spinsterish-looking secretary poked her head timidly into the office. "For two. Get us some sandwiches. They're harder to ruin than the daily special."

Looking as though she might be held personally responsible for the bad cooking, the girl withdrew. Kerr traded a butt for a fresh cigarette and started talking. Gallant didn't bother taking notes. His memory was not of pachydermal proportions, but it would serve. Besides, Kerr's pace was too rapid.

"Bowmanville," Kerr continued, "has an appropriate background for its present usage. It used to be a reformatory for boys. Since it's a permanent installation, the facilities are rather good. In fact, it's known as the most luxurious POW camp in existence. They call it the 'U-boat Hotel.' Eighty percent of the POWs at Bowmanville are U-boaters. The others are half air force, half Rommel's boys from Africa. It is an officers' camp. There's one company of enlisted personnel to do the work for them. Officers don't work in prison camps. Geneva Convention rules. You probably know that.

"In general we bend over backwards to observe the rules of the Geneva Convention. The shackling case was an exception —a justifiable one in my opinion. It was a necessary reprisal to enforce observance of the rules by the Germans. They don't have our compunctions. It would be a damn sight easier on us if we could follow suit more often. Our leniency can be quite costly at times. Unless one enforces absolutely throttling restrictions, prisoners are bound to be up to all sorts of tricks. Escapes. Even sabotage."

Miss Griffon knocked discreetly at the door and was told to enter. She set a tray covered by a napkin on Kerr's desk and crept out again. She obviously had been trained. Kerr abhorred being fussed over. He ignored the food and continued his discourse. Gallant unveiled the tray and helped himself to a sandwich.

"We know approximately what to expect in the way of undercover activities in any camp. Since we can't stamp them out, our main concern is to see that they don't get out of hand. And that's just what I'm afraid might be happening at Bowmanville."

Gallant took a bite out of his sandwich, shook his head sorrowfully and put the rest back on his plate.

"You've killed all my ambition, Kerr," Gallant joshed. "I thought I'd plug along till I made general, but if they can't do you any better than this . . ." He indicated the soggy sandwiches.

"Wait till you get to Bowmanville," Kerr promised. "The cuisine is ten times better than in this benighted madhouse."

"If it isn't, I can see why they'd be driven to escaping," Gallant answered.

"All prisoners—no matter where or what kind—dream of escaping," Kerr replied seriously. "You might say it's an occupational disease. And the actual planning of an escape is occupational therapy. It's a complicated business, takes a lot of ingenuity and hard work.

"At any rate, no matter which, dreaming about it or actively organizing it, an escape plan makes the abnormal life in prison bearable for a man. It gives his sterile existence an objective.

"There are exceptions and I daresay they all convince themselves they have lofty motives—patriotism, duty—but for the most part, they're young men and they're driven by the same motivation that has always made the world go 'round. I think it's the tail that wags the dog. We've picked up more escapees in whorehouses than hotfooting it on the trail home.

"Of course, here in Canada there's little likelihood of their getting home. The Atlantic Ocean's too big a puddle. There are a few who have never been recaptured, but to my knowledge only one ever made it home. That was in the early days of the war while the States and Mexico were still neutrals. He managed to cross the States and get to his consulate in Mexico City. He was repatriated."

"What percentage actually manage to pull off an escape?" Gallant asked.

"There are no official figures. But very, very few. Most of them are tripped up somewhere along the line, before they can set their plans into action. A periodic surprise inspection will uncover their escape tools, tunnels or civilian clothing.

"Bowmanville may have a slightly higher escape rate than other camps because of the caliber of the men it houses. For one thing, they're the elite, the special services—submariners, aviation and the Afrika Korps. What's more, many of them come from Grizedale Hall. Grizedale's the place for the bad boys in the old country. It's a castle, used to be one of the stately homes of England. Now it's a maximum-security prison. The habitual escapees usually wind up there.

"I mentioned before that we know approximately what to

expect in the way of undercover activity. Let me give you a rundown on that.

"In all camps—ours and theirs—the prisoners establish a complete microcosm of their own. They all operate both internal and external intelligence services. In some respects internal intelligence serves the detaining power as well and it's tolerated unofficially.

"There are broad areas of activity which must be organized and regulated by the prisoners themselves. The commanding officer of the prisoners rules his men in much the same manner inside the camp as he would outside and he keeps his finger on the pulse of the camp by his intelligence service. It's his job, in other words, to keep his men in line. It works out to everyone's advantage. The detaining power is spared a lot of bother and the prisoners are more content being disciplined by their own people.

"It may sound like a strange setup, but it is well justified. In one case, for instance, the inside CO discovered that some of his men were plotting to murder the camp commandant. He put a quick stop to that." Kerr chuckled. "Not cricket to do away with COs, even enemy ones. If we die with our boots on, it's only because we wear them to bed.

"The POWs' internal intelligence service also keeps tabs on the military record of each man and of any cases of mistreatment or of breaches of the Geneva Convention. That's about as far as their legitimate functions go. Sub rosa, internal intelligence also rides herd on traitors, troublemakers and political agitators: the Schröders, in other words. As far as we know, it's extremely rare that they'll go as far as liquidating a man in a camp. But I'm sure they have their little list for after the war—if they win.

"External intelligence is a strictly illicit undertaking. By and large it is divided into three sections: psychological, supply and operational." Kerr ticked them off on his fingers.

"The first is undoubtedly the one we've just been confronted with in Bowmanville. To put it in simple terms, the function of the psychological group is to determine exactly how much the prisoners can get away with. The group makes what's known in the field as a continuing and progressive analysis of the character, intellectual horizon and the habits and weaknesses of the camp commandant, his staff officers and noncoms. The object is to guess how they will react to any given situation.

"I use the word 'guess,'" Kerr interjected. "The self-proclaimed experts in psychological warfare would consider that bad form. They would insist on 'predict' or 'determine.'"

"I know," Gallant agreed. "I had a few dealings with the experts myself. What was the outcome at Bowmanville? Did they guess right?"

"That's one of the things I expect you to tell me," Kerr answered. "From now on, among other things, you are my expert on psychological warfare.

"To all appearances, Bowmanville was a stalemate since the issue was settled before the riot ended. Colonel Perry might even be one up since he avoided the use of real force—firearms, that is—and he had the prisoners pretty well in control at the end. But until we know what the objective of the riot was, we can't be sure who won.

"To go on," Kerr pursued his lecture, "the psychological group tries to dope out if, when and how officers may be blackmailed into making concessions. They may try to discover, say, if the CO is at odds with Ottawa and risks being relieved in case of trouble. The group also probes for dishonesty, weaknesses and idiosyncrasies among the NCOs."

"Do they assume, then, that only NCOs, and not officers, are capable of dishonesty?"

"I never thought of that," Kerr answered. "Perhaps it's a reflection of the Junker code, although I shouldn't think the Nazis subscribe to that. At any rate, the fact is we've never had an officer report an attempted bribe. That doesn't necessarily mean they weren't made. The NCOs do report them fairly frequently. With all due respect to the lower echelons, we still have to presume there are some who accept."

"And with all due respect," Gallant added, "perhaps the NCOs get the offers because they're in more immediate contact with the prisoners."

"The defense rests," Kerr quipped.

"Now, as for the two other external-intelligence groups, supply and operations, they're concerned almost exclusively with the business of escaping. All projected escapes are supposed to be approved by the commanding officer. Once he puts his okay on an idea, the escapee can apply for help in carrying it out.

"First, he goes to supply, which enlists the help of all inmates in procuring and storing prohibited articles. In a community of almost a thousand men, it's possible to procure or actually to manufacture almost any necessary object. There are specialists to be found on just about everything—engineers, chemists, tailors, radiomen, shoemakers. You name it and nine chances out of ten there's someone who can do it.

"It's amazing that they can get the raw materials, but they're devilishly ingenious about making something out of nothing. Every scrap they get their hands on goes to some use. They've made radios, compasses, special inks, even special papers for counterfeiting identity documents. If an item is absolutely unobtainable here, they try to smuggle it in. We've found things in Red Cross food parcels, bookbindings, sewed into clothing. Some of the stuff appears to be sent automatically. They've probably drawn up a list of escapees' needs in Berlin. At times we've also discovered coded messages requesting special materials. And it goes without saying that, whenever a permanently disabled man is repatriated on the prisoner-exchange program, he carries a list of messages back with him. There's no way to stop that particular dodge.

"Actually, it's becoming increasingly difficult for them. The war's been on enough years now so that we have rather precise knowledge of their *modus operandi*. They do come up with new tricks all the time but, by and large, I should say we're increasing our edge on them.

"Now, as for the third group—operations—among other things it takes care of the coding I just mentioned. It also produces maps, gets hold of timetables, charts, freight-train schedules, and counterfeits official forms and identity papers."

Kerr looked at his watch and shoved the tray of uneaten food away.

"Lunch hour's over. I've given you about all the dope there is. From now on it's your problem. Feel your way around down there. Give it what you think it's worth," Kerr summed up in newspaper jargon.

CHAPTER 4

Modersohn sat at the head of the refectory table which had been made at his express order in the camp carpentry shop. At the other end sat von Westhofen, gray and fragile-looking, with Linke, a pale reflection of the general, at his right. To Modersohn's right was von Sperle, also cast in the mold of his superior but supplementing him in fervor. A luftwaffe major, Herman Schlenker, in charge of intelligence, was installed exactly halfway down the twelve-foot length of highly varnished pine tabletop. Facing him was Colonel Georg Unger, an army engineer.

To all appearances, mused von Westhofen, the meeting had the earmarks of a joint planning session of the Afrika Korps, the kriegsmarine and the luftwaffe. In this setting it certainly didn't look like what it was: a meeting of the council of elders, the Ältestenrat, of a POW camp. The barrack room had a solid military air to it. The table befitted usage by staff officers. Only if one glanced out the window, as von Westhofen did, and noticed the machine gun in the watch tower, was the illusion destroyed. The machine gun faced the wrong way: inward instead of outward.

But von Westhofen had no illusions left anyway. Not even that he was doing his duty. He was merely going through the motions decreed by his trade and traditions. He was no longer leading, even symbolically. Modersohn was making that clear.

"General von Westhofen," the naval captain said, his voice a monotone, without coloring or emotion, "you shall have to inform the camp commandant that you are stepping down as our commanding officer and that I am taking your place. You, of course, understand the necessity for this move."

Von Westhofen nodded his assent. To all intents and purposes he had not been commanding officer since Modersohn arrived at Bowmanville nine months previously.

"I regret making you bear the onus, General," Modersohn elaborated diplomatically for the others, "but the camp commandant will be more amenable if he has a scapegoat to present to the authorities in Ottawa. Particularly in view of the Schröder episode. His complaint will weaken our otherwise justifiable action against this illegal shackling. We shall, of course, deny anything Schröder has to say."

"I shall be allowed, I presume," von Westhofen replied, his reedy voice containing a barely perceptible tone of irony, "to plead ill health as the reason for my resignation."

"Naturally, General," Modersohn answered, noting but not perturbed by the general's asperity. The general had no further usefulness, neither in the camp nor in the future of Germany. He was too old, too *vieux jeu.*

"Major Schlenker," Modersohn addressed the intelligence officer, "you will take the necessary steps with regard to Schröder. Warnings to all POW camps. He is to be isolated from all activity and contacts, but not molested. We don't want any repercussions at this particular stage."

"Berlin will have his record, too," the major replied righteously. "They'll deal with him later, I assure you. No traitor to our Fatherland will go unpunished."

Although his face remained expressionless, Modersohn winced inwardly, not for Schröder's fate but because of the need to tolerate Schlenker's presence. Modersohn prided himself as an intellectual snob. The Schlenkers were good work horses, necessary to the military machine, but they did not grace one's table.

"Gentlemen," Modersohn glanced at each man in turn, communicating to them the import of what he was about to say, "the moment has come for you to be informed of a historic event. I have received word today from Admiral Doenitz, who, as you know, has taken over command of the navy from Admiral Raeder, that he is approving a project we have been discussing by letter. From now on this project will have top priority in Bowmanville and I shall require the cooperation of every man in the camp.

"You will understand," he continued diplomatically, "that I could not reveal these plans prematurely. It was not for lack of faith in you. In wartime we all sail under sealed orders. Security is security."

And Doenitz is Doenitz, the Afrika Korps general thought. *The submarine arm has always been his favorite and Silent Willi is the ace of the U-boaters, the captain with the most enemy tonnage to his credit. Which explains why Berlin gave orders for this naval underling to take precedence over me. Doenitz came into command in January and immediately started politicking for his pets.*

As if to corroborate von Westhofen's thoughts, Modersohn continued: "Some of us here in Bowmanville constitute Germany's most important strategic reserve. I refer to the U-boat commanders and executive officers. This is not a partisan belief. I want you to listen to me closely now so that you understand it is for unselfish motives I am demanding your entire cooperation.

"Our Fatherland's main hope of concluding this war advantageously is to stop the Allied troops before they set foot on the continent of Europe. This means sinking their freighters and troop ships."

Interesting thought von Westhofen. *Not even this wheel horse speaks of winning. He talks of concluding advantageously.*

"Admiral Doenitz had convinced the Führer to give top priority to our submarine construction program," Modersohn related.

"Germany has the industrial capacity to construct sufficient U-boats to give us command of the seas. We need experienced captains to man them. Admiral Friedeburg is doing a first-rate job training new crews and skippers, but there is no substitute for experience. At the present moment we are losing U-boats faster than we are replacing them. This is because the new boats now going out are frequently commanded by officer-cadets, some of them as young as the class of 1939."

His face stern, Modersohn paused to look directly at each of his listeners.

"I am giving you these facts—top-secret facts—to impress on you the absolute necessity for the success of my project. If we cease to attack Allied communications at sea, the war is as good as lost. I have this from Admiral Doenitz himself.

"The only men with the experience to perform this vital task are in the prison camps. They are our Fatherland's secret strategic reserve. With these men lies Germany's main hope. It only remains to put them into action. That is what I propose to do.

"With Leutnant von Sperle, I have selected twenty-six U-boat officers—the cream of Bowmanville and of the kriegsmarine too, I might add—who will join us in sweeping Allied shipping from the seas.

"We are going to return to the Fatherland, gentlemen. Twenty-eight experienced commanders to lead our new wolf packs.

"We shall carry on in the tradition of our immortal heroes: Gunther Prien and Joachim Schepke."

All five officers listening to Silent Willi's unprecedented histrionics knew the saga of Prien and Schepke. It was also the saga of Modersohn. It had passed into the folklore of the German navy.

Early in March 1941, Prien, Schepke and Modersohn, Hitler's three ace U-boat commanders, met in occupied France at the Lorient submarine base. By coincidence, for the first time in their careers, all three were to put out on a cruise on the same day. The evening before they set sail, the three skippers made a wager as to which one would be the first to sink 300,000 tons of enemy shipping. The prize was to be a champagne dinner.

All three commanders were near the 300,000-ton mark. Modersohn led with 282,000 tons. Runnerup Prien, with 245,000 tons, had the most fabled exploit to his credit. It was Prien who sneaked his U-boat through the nets into the British fleet anchorage at Scapa Flow and sank the battleship *Royal Oak* at her moorings.

Schepke, low man among the three, had a creditable 230,000 tons chalked up.

A few days out of Lorient, on March 10, Prien attacked an

inward-bound convoy some two hundred miles south of Iceland. Running on the surface under the cover of the blustery North Atlantic winter weather, he harried the edges of the convoy, counting on sighting before being sighted, a tactic favoring the low-silhouetted U-boats.

Emerging suddenly from the obscurity of a rain squall, Prien's U-42 found itself face to face with the destroyer *HMS Wolverine*. Prien ordered a crash dive and tried to sit out the subsequent depth-charging.

After sustaining much damage, its hull cracked and taking water, the U-42 made for the surface, where Prien decided to take advantage of the low visibility to run for it.

One mile away from where the U-42 surfaced, the *Wolverine* lay in wait. Her asdic picked up the throb of the sub's props and the destroyer resumed the chase. Unable to outrun or out-fight the British vessel, Prien chose to dive again rather than surrender. More depth charges sought him out, this time crushing the U-42's hull. She was lost with all hands.

Two nights later, Schepke also lost his chance to collect the wager. His U-100, one of a wolf pack of five, made contact with a convoy and accounted for a 10,000-ton tanker, the *Erodna*. Shortly afterward, five more ships fell victim to the wolf pack's torpedoes but not without the escort vessels' closing in.

The U-100 was picked up on an asdic fix and a depth charge pattern dropped around its position. Schepke managed to worm through, apparently without damage, and three hours later came up to pursue the convoy once more.

The destroyer *Vanoc* caught the U-100 on the surface at close quarters and headed for it on collision course. Rammed by the *Vanoc*, the U-100 went for its last dive, taking all aboard with it.

The story of Modersohn's last action was much more obscure, although almost the whole crew was alive to tell the tale if they chose.

A short time after the U-100 went down, Modersohn's U-125, on its way home after expending all its torpedoes, ran into the convoy Schepke had tangled with. It was night and the U-125 was cruising on the surface with von Sperle in charge on the deck.

Standing orders in such a situation were for a U-boat to run away on the surface, where it stood a better chance of speeding to safety. For a reason never revealed, von Sperle gave orders to dive.

The asdic of the convoy-escort group spotted the submerged U-125 and the destroyer *Walker* quickly overtook and depth-charged it. At that point the U-125 elected to surface. It came up, unhappily, directly astern of the *Vanoc,* the ship which had sunk the U-100 a few hours before. Searchlights pinpointed Modersohn's craft and both destroyers started shelling it.

Its signal lamp flashing the distress signal "We are sinking," the U-125 struck its colors. Most of the crew were saved, Modersohn being the last man to be picked up.

True to his name, Silent Willi never explained the last hour of his boat's life. It could only be surmised that he didn't hold von Sperle at fault since he was still acting as his second. And who could blame Modersohn for choosing to live rather than going to the bottom with his command?

Waves of pink flushed the face of Colonel Unger as his blood coursed patriotically at the remembrance of the heroism of the U-boat skippers.

"You may count on every man in this camp, sir," he enthused. "I know I can speak for all. Think what it will mean. Twenty-eight experienced skippers, each one of a caliber to sink 300,000 tons. It would be a sure victory."

Von Westhofen cast an icy glance at the engineering officer. It was dismaying to find a field-grade officer with so little discernment and so much naïveté. Those record sinkings had been achieved in the early days of the war before the Allies had the equipment and the experience to take countermeasures. Now the tables were turned. Modersohn's implication notwithstanding, it wasn't only the inexperienced new crop of U-boat skippers which accounted for the appalling U-boat casualty rate.

In von Westhofen's opinion, there was only one hope for Germany: a negotiated truce. But to bring that about, one had to show the enemy one was still powerful. In that light, the building up of the U-boat fleet made sense. And Modersohn's plan could contribute to making that arm more effective—if it worked.

Von Westhofen wasn't the only officer around that pine table who had reservations about the plan's practicality once their initial enthusiasm gave way to thought. To break out of a prison camp *en masse* was difficult, but possible. But to envisage a return to the Continent from Canada—with three thousand miles of ocean to cross—was fantasy. Yet, under that granite exterior, Silent Willi was fantastic too, in a different sense of the word. He was a man to accomplish the impossible.

The other officers waited patiently for Modersohn to continue. The Afrika Korps general was the only one who dared interrupt the U-boat ace's systematic narration to challenge him.

"I'm sure, my dear Kapitän," the Junker's tone was haughty, "you've planned this operation well. Please explain to us how you propose to accomplish the repatriation of your strategic reserves."

I'm afraid we're out of favor with the man who knew how to walk on water, he thought of adding.

A tiny smile played on Silent Willi's thin lips as he answered: "By submarine."

"Of course, how natural," said Unger.

"Wonderful," said Schlenker.

"One submarine for twenty-eight men?" queried the general. "Where will you put them? I was under the impression space aboard U-boats is almost as limited as in tanks."

"Admiral Doenitz has agreed to send a U-boat tanker. They are roomier than attack boats.

"As I was about to tell you, we must decide on the date and the place for our rendezvous with the tanker. This must be done today. My reply will go out in tonight's mail in order to allow the admiral a maximum of time to arrange his fleet operations and to inform us if his schedule can accommodate our proposal.

"Leutnant von Sperle has all the details of our escape plan. I will leave him to consult with you on the precisions of working out a schedule. Remember, gentlemen, top priority. All other matters are to be suspended.

"General," Modersohn stood up, "will you please accompany me. I have arranged a meeting with Colonel Perry to submit your resignation. It is time, is it not, von Sperle?"

"Exactly, sir."

Erect, gray-faced, as though he were being marched to his own execution, von Westhofen left the room, Modersohn one pace behind him. Von Sperle was already carrying on.

"Colonel Unger, I shall need your technical corroboration of our plans."

"Of course, my dear von Sperle."

"We are going to take over the tunnel which the group in Barrack III is digging. You are familiar with it, I believe."

Unger nodded.

"Do you think that's fair?" Linke interrupted, instinctively trying to protect the men in his branch of service. "Those men have been digging for over half a year. They aren't submariners so I suppose you won't take them with you."

"No, we won't take them with us. But they may use the tunnel after us. The more the merrier, Kapitän Linke. It'll confuse the bloodhounds. The only condition is our group gets first claim on all materials needed for the escape."

"You'll scrape the bottom of the barrel to equip twenty-eight men," Linke said accusingly.

"Military priority." Von Sperle laughed and then added pompously: "We are going someplace. What does the other group plan to do when it gets out?"

"Sabotage."

"Yes, they'll knock up some whores in a Montreal brothel.

"Now," von Sperle returned to the matter at hand after laughing at his own sally, "the tunnel is two hundred and twenty feet long already. We need to bring it out to a point one hundred fifty feet beyond the wall. You don't mind my calculating in feet instead of meters, do you, Colonel? The men have been using a Canadian tape measure requisitioned from the tailoring shop."

"When in Rome, my dear fellow . . ."

"Fine then. We want to bring the tunnel out one hundred and fifty feet beyond the wall because there is a dip in the ground at that point which will allow us to get out without being seen from the observation tower.

"According to our calculations, we have two hundred seventy feet more to dig: that is, thirty feet more to the trip wire, ninety feet from there to the wall plus the hundred and fifty feet to our exit point. Do you follow me, Colonel?"

"Yes, yes. Your figures are quite accurate."

"I know," von Sperle said smugly. "Here is where I want your technical approval. Kapitän Modersohn and I estimate that we can complete the tunnel in three months."

Unger started to throw up his hands in protest.

"Wait till I've finished, Colonel. We will operate on a round-the-clock basis. Heretofore the excavation has been proceeding on one eight-hour shift."

"But there are many technical problems to be overcome," the colonel objected. "The disposal of the soil, for one. That's always the biggest problem. On this particular job the whole barrack has cooperated to carry the soil outside in their pockets and spread it around so it may not be noticed. Even now the method is proving unsatisfactory. It will certainly be inadequate for larger amounts of earth."

"We've taken that problem into consideration, naturally. The excavated soil will be stored in the space between the ceiling and the roof of Barrack III. There's no normal use of that area and it has never been the object of an inspection."

"That would seem to be a sound idea. I shall have to calculate the structural strength of the ceiling. We may need to add supports.

"That's your province, my dear Unger. I'm glad to see it is in competent hands."

"There are other logistics to be considered as well," the mollified engineering officer added. "Timber to shore up the tunnel, for instance and . . ."

"Supply will be taken care of by Kapitän Linke as usual. I'm sure we can count on him to do the impossible."

"You'll have your timber, Colonel, even if I have to strip all the bed boards in camp," Linke promised, caught up in the fever of the project.

Von Sperle welcomed Linke to the team with an approving smile.

"We've also thought of using other standard mining practices to speed up the operation," the U-boat officer continued. "We'll want a ventilation system. With more men working and the length of the tunnel increasing, we shall need more oxygen.

"We are also going to install a trolley in the mine and in the attic to move the dirt rapidly. And a concealed elevator to hoist it from the tunnel to the attic.

"These are engineering and supply problems which we will

let you gentlemen work out in due time. What Kapitän Moder-sohn wants to know from you today, Colonel, is whether you see any reason the job can't be completed in three months."

"Hm," Unger cleared his throat, seeking time before commit-ting himself. He wanted both to please and to perform mira-cles. Above all, he considered himself a patriotic German. But he also was a competent and conscientious engineer and his loyalty wasn't so blind as to color the facts.

"It's a tight schedule. Very tight. The improvements you sug-gest will help but there is no leeway for imponderables—acci-dents, breakdowns, maybe changes in the composition of the strata, harder soil, rock formations. I can almost predict we will run into every one of these situations. We could even have a cave-in or be flooded out entirely by an underground spring."

"Let's not go into consideration of matters that are beyond our control, Colonel. I agree, though, we must allow leeway for what you call the 'imponderables.' "

"There is only one solution," Unger answered, encouraged by von Sperle's seeming agreement. "More time. We must delay the rendezvous. You cannot force nature."

Von Sperle walked to the window and stared at the distant wall as though willing it to crumble. Modersohn had studied the schedule and decided it was feasible. It was his duty to see that no stone was left unturned in implementing it.

"Colonel," von Sperle said incisively, "I have found that there is one exception to the laws of the universe: man. As you say, we may run into innumerable delays. Time may be lost because of accidents, broken tools, any number of physical rea-sons. They are not flexible—but man is. All other factors in a situation may be unchangeable, but man can always be called upon to expend himself a little more. There is your safety mar-gin. The crews will work harder to step up our production rate."

"But I thought the schedule was already calculated on maximum production."

"The old maximum, my dear chap. We shall establish a new one. Man always betters his time. We see examples of that every day in sports. Man runs faster, jumps higher, lifts heavier weights at each Olympic. This time he will dig faster."

CHAPTER 5 The jeep driver who picked up Gallant at the railroad station in the town of Bowmanville the following morning saluted respectfully, recognizing in him the mark of a combat officer. After installing his traveled duffel bag on the rear seat, the Veterans' Guard private drove his passenger smartly out of town and north along Highway 2, looking for an opportunity to engage him in conversation. It wasn't often one saw a man who'd been overseas in this war on the right side of the fence in Bowmanville.

Gallant ignored the old soldier's inquisitive glances and concentrated on the landscape. Leaving the shore of Lake Ontario, the jeep drove through gently rolling countryside planted in apple orchards and pine forest. After a mile and a half it turned off the highway onto a side road, bounced along another half mile through a forest before coming to a well-tended farm area bordered by a split-rail fence. A post carried a warning sign: "MILITARY AREA, NO ADMITTANCE."

Beyond the farm rose the twelve-foot-high brick walls of the POW camp. As the jeep skirted the entranceway, an iron-barred double gate, Gallant read the eroded lettering cut in the stone above it: "BOWMANVILLE BOYS REFORMATORY."

In a clearing outside the wall opposite the gate were some long wooden buildings, little better than sheds, of temporary wartime construction.

"The colonel's office is in here," the driver directed Gallant, stopping the jeep in front of the first structure. "I'll take your bag along to officers' quarters if you'd like, sir."

Gallant thanked the man and stepped out of the jeep. In the front office he was met by a potbellied clerk in a corporal's uniform who announced him to the colonel.

"Ah, Captain Gallant," Perry greeted him, "sorry to have made you come all this way. Usually my recommendations for transfer go through automatically."

"Don't excuse yourself on my account, Colonel," Gallant answered, sizing him up as a touchy character with whom it would be better to proceed slowly. "I enjoyed the ride up here. It's worth the trip, particularly in the spring."

"It is a beautiful region," Perry agreed. "I suppose you will want to see Schröder immediately so you can get back to Ottawa, though."

"Yes, I would like to see Schröder as soon as possible. Your report, of course, was quite comprehensive, but there are a few points General Kerr has asked me to go into."

"I did try to make it complete," Perry said defensively. "I can't think of anything to add to it, but if you have any questions you'd like to put to me . . ."

"As a matter of fact, there are some questions I have to discuss with you but they only have an indirect bearing on the Schröder incident. The general didn't bring up the matter when he phoned you since he felt a public line wasn't the proper place to discuss them."

Noting suspicion in Perry's face, Gallant sought to lessen the tension with the offer of a cigarette.

"No thank you, I don't smoke," said Perry, who looked all the more irritated at Gallant as he lit up and, not finding an ashtray, dropped the match in the wastepaper basket.

"The general feels there is a possibility," Gallant continued, "that the Schröder incident and the little uprising you had here may both stem from the same source and that they may be an indication of some sub rosa activity. He's requested me to look into the situation since I'm here to interview Schröder anyway."

"I have no orders to extend you any facilities other than regarding Schröder," Perry replied stiffly. "However, I think we may be spared concern about that. I believe I know what may have prompted the general's suspicions, and the matter has been rectified. It will be in today's report, which he will undoubtedly receive in good time."

"It might help if I knew the contents of the report now. I realize it is a bit unorthodox for me to arrive here without your having been informed of the exact nature of my mission. If you want to confirm it, a telephone call will do the trick."

"Oh, I don't doubt your word, Captain," Perry backwatered. "I suppose it would expedite matters if I gave you the gist of my report now."

"Very likely."

Gallant snuffed his cigarette in the wastepaper basket with deliberation.

Joining his hands as though praying, Perry raised his eyes to the ceiling to compose his thoughts.

"You've read my earlier reports, I presume, so you are familiar with the personalities involved?"

Gallant nodded.

"Good," Perry pontificated. "General von Westhofen and Captain Modersohn requested an interview with me this morning. When they arrived here General von Westhofen asked to be relieved of his duties as senior officer of the prisoners. He is an elderly gentleman and pleaded ill health as the reason for his resignation. There was no necessity for going into the real reason. We were all aware that it was a diplomatic excuse.

"Captain Modersohn accompanied the general because he is next in line for the office, not only in regard to seniority, but also because the majority of our prisoners are in his line of service, the navy.

"I accepted the general's resignation and approved the captain as spokesman for the camp. Indeed, I might go so far as to say that the change came about at my instigation. In a previous interview, I let the general know that his conduct these past few days had irremediably impaired our working relationship. That was largely sufficient to provoke his resignation. These old Junkers have a lot of pride; frequently turn a pistol on themselves when their honor is in question."

"Then you think, Colonel, that von Westhofen was wholly to blame for the uprising?"

"That sounds like a journalist's question, young man." Perry smiled chidingly. "Don't make me go out on a limb. I don't know about 'wholly.' But I should say 'largely.' It all fits in quite well with the Prussian concept of honor, something I have the advantage of knowing from World War I. Right or wrong, the general felt strongly about his men being shackled."

"Very interesting," Gallant murmured obligingly. "How does that fit in with the purported attempt to murder Schröder?"

"I think those were two separate incidents, having nothing to do with each other. Two possible explanations of the Schröder incident have suggested themselves to me. One is that it is largely a product of his own imagination. I must admit that he does sound convincing and there were witnesses of a sort, but there's nothing conclusive in that. Prison life does bring out the neurotic side of a man.

"The other explanation is that some sort of feud is going on between Schröder and some brother officers. Petty squabbles of all sorts erupt in prison and are magnified beyond all reason.

"But go see Schröder yourself, Captain. I'll be interested to know what you make of him."

Seldom required for the disciplining of the mature Veterans' Guard troops, the cell block of the Bowmanville guardhouse consisted of only one cage partitioned off from the office by heavy wire netting. Schröder lay on one of the two cots in the cell reading a copy of *Maclean's Magazine*. The scene reminded Gallant of innumerable small-town lockups he had visited in the course of his newspaper days. Except for his uniform, Schröder appeared like any young man bored by his incarceration, passing the time until his trial date.

Schröder looked up apathetically when the key clanged in the lock of the cell door. Seeing an officer enter, he got to his feet. Gallant presented himself.

"Cigarette?" he offered.

"Thank you, Captain," Schröder accepted. Gallant proferred a match, trying in the short interval to make an intuitive judgment on Schröder, but he looked no different than any other German flyer he had seen or imagined.

"Hardly an improvement for you being locked up in here. I imagine you had more freedom in the camp," Gallant said, seating himself on the spare cot and waving Schröder to the other.

"Freedom, Captain? I had the freedom to walk around, if that's what you mean. I also had the freedom to follow or to die. Not to disagree. Like in the Fatherland."

"Lieutenant Schröder, I've been sent down here to decide what to do about your complaint," Gallant answered. "It may seem harsh to you, but it is difficult for us to believe your sudden change of heart. Or should I say 'mind'?"

"It may be that they are connected, Captain, the heart and the mind."

Too glib an answer, my boy, Gallant thought.

"They may be, Schröder, but that's not what I want to discuss. Frankly, you're more of a problem to us as a reformed character than as an unreconstructed Nazi. We haven't any provisions for safeguarding you. I don't know where we could keep you. Perhaps in a jail someplace. Not a very pleasant prospect, particularly if the war lasts a long time."

Schröder opened his hands in a gesture of resignation, apparently willing to accept solitary confinement to a return to the prison compound.

"Perhaps it would be safe for you to stay in Bowmanville now." Gallant was offering him an opportunity to recant. "General von Westhofen is no longer senior officer. With a new commander, I imagine policy will change. Captain Modersohn isn't likely to carry out the old edicts of von Westhofen."

"Captain Modersohn," Schröder snorted. "Is he the new commanding officer?"

"Yes, and as I understand it, the change is a welcome one to the majority of the men."

"Modersohn." The leutnant frowned. "Do you know who Modersohn is? He's the hero of the kriegsmarine. The U-boat ace. Doenitz's darling. He's more Nazi than *Mein Kampf.*

"*Himmel.*" He struck his brow. "I'm an idiot. It's only since about the time Modersohn got here—about nine months ago— that von Westhofen has been acting like a party man. There's a connection there. I'm sure of it. Before, von Westhofen was a spit-and-polish Junker, but he never would have condoned, much less initiated, a revolt against the camp authorities."

"What sort of connection, Lieutenant? Von Westhofen was still the superior officer. How could Modersohn influence his decisions?"

"Captain Gallant," Schröder said bluntly, "you haven't told me, but I guess you are an intelligence officer. You want to see how much information I am willing to supply. All right. I am quite willing to talk. But you must know yourself the role of the party in Germany. A man who stands in good with that party is more powerful than an old-line general."

Gallant smiled his acquiescence.

"If Modersohn is commanding officer now, it confirms my death sentence. His first officer was my prosecutor and Modersohn was behind him."

"Do you really think Modersohn or anyone else would risk murdering a man in an Allied prison camp?"

"It would be an accident, Captain."

"Not when it's known you warned us. It would be too risky."

"It's been done before. Do a little research in the records, if you don't believe what I am going to tell you. In 1941, shortly after Modersohn was captured, four officers escaped from a camp in England where he was. They were on a mission to sabotage the British fleet in Scapa Flow. Three of the officers were recaptured in the area before they could do anything. The fourth decided not to go through with it. He surrendered and confessed. He named Modersohn as the man behind the plot. That was when Modersohn was sent to Grizedale Hall."

Grizedale was the only thing that rang a bell to Gallant. He recalled Kerr's saying that it was a special security camp for difficult prisoners.

"The man who surrendered was found dead—hanged—a month later. They said it was suicide. But it wasn't. He was murdered. Even though he was transferred to another camp, they got him. The word went out. It's like the Mafia, Captain. There are tentacles everywhere and they get you."

"How do you know all these details? I thought you weren't in the inner circle."

"That's just why I do know. The man who was murdered—Leutnant Frolich—was my bunkmate for the last month of his life. He wouldn't have committed suicide. I know."

Schröder spoke with conviction, his torso bent slightly forward, his eyes opened wide. As he himself suggested, his story could be checked at least in part, Gallant reflected, and therefore was undoubtedly for the most part true. Unfortunately, it was a certainty that no one had ordered an autopsy on Frolich. Death was the business of war. It struck no one as an irregularity, no matter the form it came in.

No, there would be no proof of the cause of Frolich's death. Only Schröder's word and that had come suspiciously late. Why hadn't Schröder spoken up at the time? Why had he let a friend's murder go unpunished? And even before that, if Schröder had really deserted because he at last recognized Hitler's Germany for what it was, why hadn't he cooperated earlier?

Before leaving for Bowmanville, Gallant had read a copy of Schröder's interrogation when captured. He had been picked up by an air-sea rescue boat after crashing in the Channel, that much was true. But there was no proof of his having crashed voluntarily and he had refused to give any more than the required name, rank, and serial number response when questioned. Gallant wanted an explanation for his tardy about-face. He decided to try a direct approach.

"Schröder, you said just now you are quite willing to talk. Why weren't you willing to talk when you were picked up? Or when Frolich was murdered?"

Schröder rose from the cot on which he was seated to place himself on the same level as Gallant, who had gotten up to stand with his elbow on the ledge of the high, small cell window.

"When I ditched my plane, I intended to cooperate fully with the Allied authorities. I can remember just before hitting, I had all sorts of visions of how I would help the Allies and maybe . . . well, maybe almost be treated like a hero. A juvenile sort of daydream.

"And then I found myself being picked up and the crew of the boat wanted to kill me. The skipper stopped them. I didn't speak English much then, but I understood. They were mad because a German flyer they picked up the day before stabbed one of their shipmates. And then the bombings were pretty bad, too, and they were blaming me for taking part in them.

"I can understand their reaction now, but then—at the moment—it sort of made me freeze up. I'd been like that before, that's one of the reasons I deserted. I just wanted to divorce myself from the whole human race. I was so disgusted by what people in Germany were capable of doing I didn't want any contact with human beings at all. Finally I persuaded myself other peoples must be different. But when that crew wanted to tear me apart, it made me shrink back into my shell again. I didn't want to have anything to do with anyone.

"Can you understand that?"

Gallant nodded noncommittally. Schröder appeared sincere, but it wasn't his role to play the sympathetic audience.

"And what about Frolich? You'd had time to readjust by then."

"Frolich was something else. Frolich spoke and he was murdered. The camp authorities weren't able to protect him. Why should I believe they would do any better for me? I was afraid to go to them.

"And before you ask why I don't feel the same way now, let me tell you. I was placed in a position here where I couldn't sit things out any more. I was ordered to act, to go along with those Nazis in their uprising against the camp authorities. I couldn't do that and . . . Well, you know the rest. Here I am. No choice in the matter."

Schröder's story was plausible, his manner particularly convincing, yet Gallant felt somewhat like the crew of the rescue boat: he was hesitant about accepting the word of a German. On the other hand, he also, like the MO, nourished a hope that he might discover one day at least one German who didn't fall into the usual pattern. However, that was a purely personal matter and had nothing to do with the business at hand. Sincere or not about his motivations, Schröder seemed to be telling the truth about Modersohn and that's what counted.

"Looks like the good captain played me for a fool," Perry said lightly to cover his consternation on hearing Gallant's account of the interview. "That is, if Schröder can be believed," he added, clutching at a straw.

"I think he can. At any rate, we can't afford not to believe him."

"I suppose you're right."

Speculating on Perry's change of manner since their first meeting, Gallant fished a cigarette out of his pocket. Perry opened a drawer, took a crystal ashtray out of it, and placed it on the desk next to Gallant. It was an ashtray reserved for honored guests—VIPs. Gallant had entered the office expecting Perry to show resentment at the revelation of his blunder in accepting Modersohn. He certainly had resented Gallant's arrival, seeing in it an intrusion and a threat to his security. His reasonable attitude now seemed to indicate more intelligence than Gallant had given him credit for. Perry apparently recognized Modersohn as a greater potential threat to the order of his establishment than Gallant.

"What do you propose, Captain?" Perry questioned. "What can we do?"

"For the moment, nothing. I'd like to feel my way around a bit for a day or two. Of course, I'll recommend that Schröder be transferred immediately. If you can supply me with a cubbyhole and a telephone, I'll call Ottawa and arrange it."

"Of course. I'll have the corporal show you an office where you can work. But how about Modersohn? I can't remove him as senior officer without a valid reason. Schröder's claims, even if they are true, can't very well be substantiated. I suppose the best course would be to move Modersohn to another camp. I certainly don't want him in Bowmanville as senior officer."

"I agree that would be the best course eventually. But for the moment, I'd like you to hold off. If Modersohn has any other little projects, we'll never find out about them by transferring him."

"Is it necessary? We'd be nipping him in the bud and that's what counts."

"Is it? Maybe I'm a vindictive man, Colonel, but if Modersohn is the type of person who would sentence Frolich to death, I'd like to pin something on him."

"Seems a bit late for that. And remember, prisoners of war aren't criminals. We have to treat them with kid gloves."

"Prisoners of war aren't criminals, but some criminals are prisoners of war. I think you'll find that, in the thinking of many responsible parties nowadays, man should be held responsible for his acts even in wartime."

"Now you sound like a dedicated man, Captain," Perry observed, not without approval. "I'll agree to postpone Modersohn's transfer for a few days, but if the safety of my camp is threatened, I'll have to take the viewpoint that it is more important than any other consideration."

Installed in a cubicle at the other end of the building, Gallant placed a phone call to Kerr, whose rasping voice came through with the same greeting it had made for thirty years on a newspaper desk.

"Yeah, Gallant, what've you got?"

"A German who's talking. Can you send someone down to fetch him?"

"I'll have an escort there first thing in the morning. Did he give you anything we can use?"

"Not the key to Berchtesgaden, but I think he may help us prevent some more shenanigans like they had here the other day. He put the finger on the troublemaker. Character by the name of Wilhelm Modersohn, fregattenkapitän in the U-boat service and a pet of Doenitz. See what you can get on him from London. According to Schröder, he initiated a sabotage attempt on Scapa Flow by some POWs and then had one of them bumped off for backing out. Name was Gerhard Frolich. According to the record, he was a suicide. I'll send a full report down with Schröder. Take care of him, by the way. The same thing could happen to him as to Frolich. Put him in a place where he'll be safe."

"Right. I'll do what I can. But there's a housing shortage all over, you know. Even for POWs."

"This one may be the last survivor of a dying species, the good German, so try to preserve him for posterity. Say, while I think of it, you could put some of the aviation boys onto him, too. I only spoke to him about the business down here. They might get some technical stuff out of him. It may be old hat by now but at any rate he's willing to talk."

"Do you think he'd be willing to talk to the folks back home on the shortwave? Those psychological-warfare characters are always on the lookout for types like him."

"Unless he has a family back there to consider, I'd say he'd be willing."

"Right," Kerr signed off. "When you feel you've milked all you can out of it, you can go finish your leave."

CHAPTER 6   Fregattenkapitän Modersohn ran a tight ship. Not a tighter one in the U-boat service was his reputation. And the way to run a tight ship was to be everywhere and oversee everything.

At that moment, accompanied by Colonel Unger and his ADC, von Sperle, Modersohn was entering Barrack III to check the progress of the tunnel.

"Carry on, gentlemen. Look normal," he commanded those residents of the barrack who happened to be there.

The officers continued their activities with the rigidity of actors suffering opening-night stage fright. It was difficult to be relaxed with Wilhelm Modersohn as director. Two officers on sentinel duty at the front windows looked liked animated puppets in a department-store window. Modersohn glared at them.

"Relax, gentlemen. Lean on the sills, laugh, smoke, talk. Make believe you are officers in the fleet of our noble Italian allies."

The officers laughed dutifully in response to Modersohn's old canard.

"I had the day shift come out fifteen minutes early," Unger told Modersohn, "so it is clear for you to go down if you want."

The three men headed toward the full-length clothes closets which were built flush into the entire west wall of the barrack. Unger opened the door of one of the middle closets and ushered Modersohn and von Sperle in.

"Here," he said, pointing to a section of the wall in the rear of the closet. "This is a new door we installed this morning. Can't notice a thing, can you?"

He manipulated the concealed door, swinging it open and shut. Modersohn approached to inspect it, running his fingers over the seams. Fine cabinet work had made it indistinguishable from the rest of the wall.

"Unless it is measured with a tape measure," Unger boasted, "no one will be able to tell that the closet is shorter inside than out."

Modersohn opened the concealed door, looked in at the shaft illuminated by a single candle and then at the ceiling above it.

"We will cut through the ceiling the very first thing tomorrow morning," Unger hastened to say. "I have already inspected the attic."

"Structural strength?" Silent Willi snapped.

"Sufficient to support the load if the earth is distributed evenly. I inspected every square inch of the flooring myself. It is of solid construction."

"We will go down now," Modersohn stated.

Unger took some coveralls from a peg on the inside wall. The three men donned them and then, lighting another candle, Unger prepared to descend. Modersohn stopped him, took the candle and, going first, lowered himself down the ladder to the bottom, ten feet below.

"When will the electric line be in?" he inquired of Unger, who was descending after him.

"Linke says he'll have enough wire for us tomorrow to light the shaft but it'll take a few days before we get enough for the tunnel. Today he's having every spare inch of wire stripped from the installations in the barracks and, as soon as there's an opportunity, the theatrical group will procure our major requirements from the backstage supplies."

Modersohn ducked into the tunnel, his long thin body eeling its way easily. Unger followed him clumsily, straining to keep up. Von Sperle crawled along in the rear, a shadow with no reason for being there. As they penetrated deeper into the tunnel, the air became heavier, fetid. Modersohn ignored the heavy atmosphere. Choking, fearing the onset of an attack of claustrophobia, Unger struggled to reply to his questions.

"Did you check these props yourself?" Modersohn demanded, rapping on some rotten wood.

Trying to keep the panic from showing in his voice, Unger gasped: "I got a report from the digging teams themselves. They assure me the props are safe."

Modersohn ignored the gasping sounds coming from the colonel. He was aware that Unger had experienced the nightmarish ordeal of being trapped in a burning tank.

"Now you can see for yourself they are not," he answered gruffly.

Modersohn crawled on, taking satisfaction in making Unger follow him the complete length of the tunnel. It would teach him the value of personal supervision in a manner he wouldn't be likely to forget. Rather than wait until they were back on the surface, Modersohn deliberately paused at the working face to give further orders.

"From now on you will have the face widened so two men can work on it together."

"Not enough air," Unger struggled to speak. "Not for two men working. Must wait till we have the air line installed."

"When will that be?"

"Depends on how many cans we can get from the mess hall. Might take a long time before there are enough cans used up to make the complete air line."

"Be inventive, Unger. Employ other materials. Rolled cardboard or even paper will do with cans to strengthen the line at intervals.

"The construction work will start tomorrow. Without excuses. Digging will not be discontinued while it is going on. No more soil is to be dumped outside. The fresh soil will be stored along the sides of the tunnel until the track for the trolley is laid. The hoist to the attic must be finished at the same time as the track. The attic trolley can go in later. Any questions?"

Unger shook his head.

"We will go back then."

At the surface the three men took off their coveralls. Modersohn snapped "Clothes brush!" at the junior officer who was on station in the closet. The officer rushed out for the required object.

"Clothes brushes, wet washrags, and towels will be kept in the closet," Modersohn ordered as the one-striper applied the clothes brush. "The officer on station here will inspect each man before allowing him out."

Followed by von Sperle, Modersohn emerged from the barrack, both as impeccable and as unruffled as when they entered.

In the observation tower at the main gate, Gallant noticed the tall, angular officer in naval uniform leaving Barrack III followed by another blue-uniformed officer almost as tall. He turned his glasses on the pair.

"That Captain Modersohn coming out of Barrack III?" he asked the guard to confirm the description he had been given.

"Yes, sir. Can't miss that one, can you?"

Gallant studied the U-boat commander. His stride indicated his determination. His face indicated nothing, would never indicate anything, Gallant imagined. Nothing, that is, except an exaggerated degree of self-control.

"Do you see General von Westhofen around anywhere?" Gallant asked. He had climbed the tower to see for himself the men he was investigating, the conditions under which they lived.

"No. You never see him around much. Stays in most of the time. Lives over there in Barrack I."

Barracks I, II and III, stretching lengthwise across the parade grounds, faced the tower in which Gallant stood, over the main gate. The four other barracks, two in a line on either side, lay in back of and at right angles to I and III. Beyond them, parallel to the first three barracks, were two long structures housing the recreation and mess halls.

"Which one is the recreation building and which, the mess hall?" Gallant inquired.

"That's the mess on the right, back there. Recreation on the left, with the tennis courts in back of it. Tennis courts, can you imagine that? They even got tennis courts. A real country club. Gymnasium, swimming pool, library, movies. Those guys got it better than we have. Look at those barracks. Solid stone and steam-heated. And we're quartered in lousy shacks made out of green lumber that warps. Temporary barracks with permanent built-in drafts, that's what we've got."

"Would you change places with them?"

"Some days I might," the guard answered, screwing up his seamed face reflectively. "If I was an officer, that is. There's one barrack of enlisted men down there. They do all the work. Run a real spit-and-polish outfit, those Krauts do. Only you know who does all the spitting and polishing!

"Yeah," the aging soldier repeated pleasurably, "some days I might. Just sit back with nothing to do, nothing to worry about. Yeah, I'd change places every day except the day I get my pass. I'm not so old I don't know what to do when I get a pass to town," he sniggered.

So much for the opinion of the man in the street, Gallant mused to himself. Freedom meant a barroom and a broad once a week on Saturday night. Maybe that was the basic cause for a lot of the unrest down there. Maybe. But the cause mattered little except insofar as someone knew how to exploit it, knew how to channel frustration into destruction.

"Look like a bunch of ants down there, scurrying around the way they do, don't they, Captain?"

They did look like ants, Gallant had to admit. But ants merely *look* as though they are scurrying around aimlessly. Really, they are purposeful. And so, he feared, were these, these warrior ants. They had stinging bites. Given the opportunity, they would swarm over you and kill you, as they had demonstrated two days ago.

Rot, reflected Gallant. *I'm thinking in Sunday-supplement clichés. Those are men down there, not ants. And they're a thousand, ten thousand, a million times more complex than ants.*

"Think they'll try something again, sir?" the guard asked, stroking the barrel of his machine gun.

"What do you think? You've been around here longer than I."

"They seem to have calmed down now. Can't tell. Maybe

they're stir crazy. Maybe just plain crazy. Most of them seem just like you and me, but when you hear how them Nazis act, makes you wonder. They could be up to anything. I don't know what's going on in this world any more. Guess I'm getting old. This is my second war."

Gallant plodded down the circular staircase of the tower, feeling the weight of his recent illness. *Second war,* he thought disgustedly. *How will I be in my second war?* He forced a spring into his step and was gratified to feel that his muscles could still respond.

So could his brain, he realized appreciatively. With sudden insight he reasoned that, for him, it wasn't a question of a second war. This one would never stop unless something was done about the Modersohns. Those creatures on the other side of the fence were playing a new game called "total war." Total war means there is never a peace. Even when the war is lost, it doesn't stop, merely hibernates while the sequel is being prepared. That was the explanation for the Bowmanville phenomenon.

No other camp had revolted on account of the shackling order because at no other camp was there a forceful enough figure to exploit the situation, a man thoroughly imbued with a totalitarian philosophy who would see life in terms of total war.

At the bottom of the staircase, Gallant cast a satisfied glance at the high brick wall. He had discovered the answers to two of the five Ws basic to any story. He knew the *who* and the *why.* Lacking were the *what, where,* and *when.* But it was axiomatic that they existed and he wasn't going to wrap up this story without them.

Back in his cubbyhole, his feet under the desk and the pile of dossiers he had requested in front of him, Gallant felt a twinge of discontent—and of doubt. He had become a chairborne soldier. Was it possible he was magnifying the import of the situation? It might be that Modersohn was merely deluding himself. That he thought he was making a contribution to total war by harassing the elderly guards of a prison camp.

Gallant swiveled his feet out from under the desk, tilted his chair back and gazed out the window at the horizon. The pattern he was seeking became clearer. Modersohn wasn't a man to be satisfied with mock objectives. No more than Gallant himself was. They both had to know they were doing something of significance. Therefore, Modersohn had an objective wider than merely upsetting the routine at a former hostel for delinquent boys in provincial Ontario.

Gallant settled back to the dossiers with renewed interest. For the moment, research and observation were his primary weapons.

The file on Modersohn didn't turn up anything Gallant hadn't known; in fact, it contained a good deal less than he knew, being largely a record of Modersohn's stay at various camps. Perhaps intelligence would have something more on him in its files.

Conscientiously, Gallant worked his way through the rest of the folders, switching on a lamp when daylight faded and forgetting about dinner. For the most part, he learned only the names, ranks, and serial numbers of Bowmanville's inhabitants. There were also medical records and occasional references to infractions of the regulations. The only details that relieved the monotony were those concerning the few who had escaped.

A luftwaffe leutnant, Helmut Muller, had changed places with an enlisted man and gotten outside the walls on a work detail. He had hidden in a ditch, eluding the guards, and somehow had made his way to Toronto, where he was found three months later in a camp for German internees. Muller's identity was revealed when a routine check was made of a group about to be repatriated under the civilian-exchange program. Muller had been one day away from boarding a neutral Swedish ship and sailing back to Germany. He refused to reveal how he had gotten into the internment camp. Obviously he had had help. Probably from one of the rare Nazi sympathizers among the Canadians of German descent. The person could never be traced.

Muller's escape gave room for thought. A determined fanatic could do considerable sabotage, particularly if he had outside help once he escaped. Modersohn was not the type to sacrifice himself, as almost every saboteur eventually must, but he might well inspire some of his juniors to undertake such acts. He had done it once before, according to Schröder. Why not again? In Canada it would be much easier than in England. It was a larger, sparsely populated country, removed from the battle zone and nor alerted to the dangers of fifth columnists.

Two escaped prisoners, Gallant noted, had never been recaptured. It wasn't known how they got out, if they had reached home, or if they were still at large in America. But it proved that a successful escape was possible.

And to support the pseudo-Freudian reasoning concerning escapes, there was another pair, Gallant chuckled as he read, who had escaped through a sewage pipe and had been recaptured in a Montreal bordello. The military police had picked them up in a routine check because they had made the mistake of choosing Canadian army uniforms as their disguise. They surrendered quietly, as the arresting officer humorously stated in his report, having already accomplished their objective.

A bugle sounded the plaintive notes of taps, and Gallant consulted his wristwatch. Ten o'clock and all he'd accomplished was to find the material for some human-interest stories. He decided to have a final session with Schröder before he was shipped out of Bowmanville.

In the guardhouse cell, Schröder was enjoying special

privileges. His light still on, he was engaged in a game of chess with the corporal of the guard, who got up apologetically when he saw the captain enter.

"It's all right, Corporal. 'Fraid I'll have to interrupt your game, though.

"You're leaving here tomorrow morning, Schröder. Don't know if anyone told you."

"Thanks, Captain. I didn't know."

"You'll be taken care of. I expect they might keep you in isolation at an interrogation center for the duration. Might be a bit dull," Gallant shrugged.

"I'm getting used to the accommodations of a private room," Schröder grinned. "The company was becoming rather wearing out there anyway."

Gallant sat down on the spare cot and leaned back on his elbows, relaxed now that he had made up his mind it was ninety-nine-percent sure Schröder was on the level.

"I've been thinking over what you told me about Modersohn. If he organized the revolt here and the sabotage attempt in England, we can take it for granted he'll try something more. I know you haven't his confidence, but you did have a chance to observe a little. I'd like to know about the other men. Whom does he trust? Work with?"

Schröder furrowed his brow, making an honest attempt to recall something which would be of use.

"Well, all the U-boat people stick pretty much together. They always do, not only here in camp. They have more *esprit de corps* than any other service, even the luftwaffe.

"Modersohn is their old man. He doesn't mingle with them, doesn't talk to anyone, but they are his men. You can feel it. In the U-boats, men learn to obey more readily because their lives depend on it. It's a habit that stays with them.

"Modersohn hardly ever gives an order directly. Most of the

time it comes from von Sperle. He was Modersohn's first lieutenant in the U-125. I suppose he trusts him as far as he's capable of trusting any man. Even a U-boat skipper has to sleep sometimes.

"Not much help to you, that, is it, Captain?" Schröder shook his head ruefully.

"Oh, there is maybe another man he would trust," he recalled. "Rednitz. Conrad Rednitz. He used to be Modersohn's first lieutenant, too, before von Sperle. Then he got his own command. Funny sort of chap. He's the shortest man in camp. Strong, though. Must have a complex about it. They say, on a dare, Rednitz wouldn't stop at anything."

Conrad Rednitz, the shortest man in Bowmanville, was at that moment giving a demonstration of his strength and tenacity. On special orders from his former commander, Rednitz was hacking away at the face of the Barrack III tunnel.

"Set the pace for me, Rednitz," Modersohn had requested. "I want to know how much a man can dig in a four-hour shift."

His compact frame an advantage in the limited space, the tiny U-boat skipper was driving himself to the utmost. Using a short, improvised crowbar, he was chopping away at the compressed earth in rhythmical, rapid strokes. The pace he was establishing was to exhaust the crews following him. It was the measure of a man's capacity and Modersohn would accept no less. It also was a challenge to the manhood of the others not to be outdone by the diminutive Rednitz. Modersohn knew how to drive his men.

CHAPTER 7 Gallant's next two days had the unreal quality of a dream in which one never quite attains an object which stays tantalizingly just beyond grasp. He was familiarizing himself with the camp under the guidance of Sergeant Delamare. The more he saw, the more positive he was that trouble was in the offing. The stage was set, the protagonists were at hand; the conclusion could only be that the play was about to commence. Yet there was nothing to put one's finger on.

As Delamare expressed the problem, it was like a forest fire. The woods were tinder dry and there could be combustion at any moment. You couldn't control either factor. The only thing you could do was keep a sharp watch and be ready to put out the fire before it spread. You had to count on having the fire, though.

"There's only one safe way to handle prisoners," Delamare declared, "but it's not practical. You'd have to lock them up some place so tight that all they could do is eat, shit, and sleep. Even then you'd have to make them eat with their bare hands off a stone floor. They'll use anything they can get their hands on to stab you in the back or dig their way out."

Gallant had met Delamare his first night in Bowmanville. Feeling hungry after his visit to the guardhouse, he had taken a jeep out of the motor pool and driven to an all-night roadhouse recommended by the corporal of the guard. Seated at the counter waiting for his order of bacon and eggs, he'd overheard the waitress address as "Del" the sergeant seated alone a few yards away from him.

"You wouldn't be Sergeant Delamare?" he inquired, remembering the name from the reports he'd read in Kerr's office.

The sergeant nodded.

"You're Robert Gallant."

It was Gallant's turn to nod, surmising that Delamare's use of his full name indicated the sergeant knew him by his newspaper by-line as well as from the camp grapevine.

"Have a drink with me?"

"Beer," Delamare told the waitress.

"The same," Gallant said and waited until the girl left before continuing. "I was going to look you up tomorrow. Understand you had a front seat at the riot."

"I was there. The scuttlebutt is that you're here to investigate it."

"This scuttlebutt getting around to the prisoners, too?"

Grinning, Delamare answered: "Probably started with them. They know more about what's going on than anyone."

"That's what I was afraid of."

The waitress returned with their drinks.

"What were those fire engines doing up at the camp the other day?" she asked Delamare familiarly.

"CO wanted a cold drink of water."

The girl laughed and walked away again.

"Nothing much I can tell you about the other day that you probably don't know already," Delamare told Gallant, "but I think I figured out something about that Lieutenant Schröder they're keeping on ice at the guardhouse."

"What about him?"

"Well, the two guys who chased after Schröder—I got a glimpse of them out of the corner of my eye—I can't identify them, but I know they were U-boat officers. That didn't seem important till I heard tonight that General von Westhofen was taking the rap for the whole business and that Modersohn was made senior officer. If von Westhofen had any dirty work to be done, he would have chosen Afrika Korps men to do it. They stick to their own."

"And Modersohn is a U-boat man," Gallant said for him.

"That's what I had in mind."

"That makes two of you. Schröder feels Modersohn is at the bottom of all this, too.

"I'll need someone to show me around the compound. Will you be free if I put in a request for you?" Gallant asked, esteeming the sergeant's capabilities.

"It'll be a pleasure," Delamare answered, sensing that his own consent was being asked, not that of the CO.

Before Gallant and Delamare were ten feet beyond the main gate, the presence of a new officer in camp was spotted and immediately reported to Modersohn. It confirmed a report he had received the day before that there seemed to be an unknown officer in the watch tower. The fact that the new officer didn't wear the Veterans' Guard insignia indicated that he wasn't cadre. Therefore, he could only be on special mission. Modersohn gave orders that his movements were to be watched and the intelligence section was to do its utmost to discover who he was and his exact status.

By that evening, Modersohn had the measure of the new officer.

Gallant appeared at the tennis courts during a tournament match which was being followed almost as avidly by the guards as by the prisoners. Only the ice-hockey matches, the national game of Canada, held more interest for the guards. The prisoners had ten ice-hockey teams and a side benefit of both sports was the opportunity they afforded to fraternize with the guards. During these relaxed moments, differences were largely forgotten.

"New face around the camp," an affable prisoner said casually to the guard standing next to him between sets.

"That's Robert Gallant," the guard answered proudly. "He was one of our top newspaper reporters before the war. Used to see his by-line almost every day. Maybe he'll write a story about us."

Intelligence's evaluation report to Modersohn was that Gallant could be in Bowmanville for one of two reasons: either he was in public relations and was doing a story on the camp or he was there as an investigator for Canadian Intelligence. The latter theory was favored. It wasn't government policy to publicize POW camps. In particular, news like that of the riot was subject to censorship although it was possible that there had been an involuntary leak and Gallant was doing a whitewash article.

After viewing the scene at the tennis courts, Delamare escorted Gallant through the workshops in the recreation building. Not much imagination was required to see that they could serve illicit ends. The printing shop, which, in the hands of skilled printers and lithographers, turned out the camp newspaper, contained all that was needed to counterfeit the papers an escaping prisoner would require. If the work could not be done on the premises themselves, the supervision was still not so stringent as to prevent supplies being smuggled out. The same went for the other facilities: the carpentry shop, the shoemaker, the tailor.

At the entrance to the library Gallant and Delamare were intercepted by an enthusiastic submarine-service two-striper, Oberleutnant Holstein, who invited Delamare "and, of course, the captain" to a dress rehearsal starting just then of the new play he was directing. The play was written by one of the prisoners and was about Canada.

"I must have your opinion about the costumes, Sergeant," Holstein pressed. "We rented them from a theatrical costumer in Montreal, but I am not sure they are authentic, like you really wear in the north woods."

"Interested in seeing the show, Captain?" Delamare deferred to Gallant.

"We'll drop by a bit later."

"But we are starting right away," the leutnant insisted.

"Doesn't matter," Delamare told him, "I'll look at the costumes later. I can't understand two words of your language anyway, so I won't miss much."

"Maybe the captain speaks German."

"We'll look in on you later," Gallant evaded.

"Very well," Holstein said, drawing a package of cigarettes from his pocket and offering them to Gallant and Delamare, who both refused. "I am sure you will find it interesting," Holstein rattled on. "We have worked very hard on this play. We may be amateurs, but we try to do productions of professional quality. That is why I want to be sure about the costumes. Every detail in our . . ."

Holstein's monologue was interrupted by some loud, angry voices and a gutteral shout of rage coming from the assembly hall located at the end of the corridor. Holstein's offer of a cigarette had been a signal to an officer stationed in the doorway to set in motion an impromptu bit of playacting.

It wasn't necessary to understand German—although Gallant did—to know that a fight was in progress. The three men dashed down the corridor. Sounds of a struggle and more shouting were coming from the assembly hall. They arrived to find the fight being enacted on the stage at the far end of the auditorium.

"Stop!" yelled Holstein in German. "Stop this immediately."

They ran toward the stage, where four men were scuffling on the floor while a fifth danced about them brandishing a stool, yelling in German, "Get out of the way! Let me get him!"

Apparently he was addressing the pair trying to pull a broad, gorilla-like individual off someone dressed in woman's clothing whom he was convincingly choking. The gorilla-like character was dressed in a checked lumberjack's shirt which he filled to the bursting point. Despite the two men tugging at his arms and the thrashing about of his victim, he maintained his strangle hold. With a sudden surge he threw aside the two men trying to restrain him. This gave the fifth man his opening. He brought the stool crashing down on the strangler's head, knocking him unconscious.

Followed closely by Delamare and the amateur director, Gallant vaulted onto the stage as the action ended. The two men who had tried to intercede in the fight helped the man dressed as a girl to sit up. His breath came in tormented gasps too realistic to be false. Red marks showed on his neck and a large bruise on his chin.

Needing help more than he did, was the unconscious barrel-chested man. Blood streamed out of a break in his scalp under his thick black hair. Still holding the stool, the man who had clobbered him stood looking dumbly at the three newcomers.

"Drop the stool," Holstein said as he and Gallant knelt at the side of the unconscious man. Gallant felt his pulse. It beat powerfully, but there was no doubt that he wasn't shamming. Holstein applied a handkerchief to staunch the blood. The man stirred, his eyes fluttering.

"Go tell the corporal of the guard to bring the doctor here immediately," Delamare ordered one of the officers.

Holstein got to his feet, glared at his actors and, to impress Gallant, berated them in German, playing the scene more for effect than comprehension.

"You idiots! Now look what you've done. You are going to ruin my play, acting like undisciplined schoolboys. I'll have you all up on charges before the Ältestenrat."

"That's enough, Lieutenant," Delamare broke in, not wanting a conversation to go on above his head. "These men are to consider themselves under arrest. You're not to have any communication with them."

"It is for the Ältestenrat to punish them," Holstein insisted. "This is a matter between prisoners."

"Colonel Perry will decide that," Delamare retorted firmly.

Skeptical about any occurrence in the camp, Gallant wanted to hear the prisoners' explanation for the set-to before they had further opportunity to discuss it among themselves.

"While we're waiting for the MO, Sergeant," he suggested, "supposing we find out what this was all about.

"Supposing you tell us," he said, turning to the officer succoring the strangled man.

Well rehearsed, the amateur thespian's eyes sparkled in revolt and his lips took on a stubborn set. It wouldn't do to appear too cooperative.

"Doesn't he speak English?" Gallant asked Holstein.

"I am not an informer," the man answered for himself, sullenly.

"It is alright, Gustav," croaked the officer dressed as a girl. "I will tell him. It was a silly quarrel. The lieutenant there"—he indicated his opponent—"could not take a joke. 'Battle fatigue' I think you call it. He is peculiar sometimes. It was my fault. I should have remembered that."

Seeing Gallant glance apprehensively at the injured man, who was sitting up with the help of Holstein, holding the handkerchief to his head, he added: "He did not understand. Does not speak English."

"What was the joke?" Gallant pursued.

"He said I would have a lot of success around camp dressed like this," the smooth-faced officer related reluctantly. "So I told him—jokingly, of course—that it was always the big strong ones who were repressed homosexuals. Then he started getting angry and I said that proved it. Next thing I knew he was choking me."

"I knocked him out," the man who wielded the stool took up, "because it was the only way to stop him. He is as strong as an ox. When he goes berserk, no one can hold him."

"Yes, he has done this before," the director of the play spoke his line.

The arrival of the MO confirmed their statements.

"Oh, that one again," he said to Gallant on seeing his patient. "He's a regular customer.

"Might be a malingerer," he added in an undertone, "trying to get on the exchange list."

"What did you think of it, Del?" Gallant asked after the MO and the corporal of the guard had herded their charges out.

"Well, I'll concede the blood was real," the sergeant shrugged. He was aware that it was common practice for

POWs to divert attention from illicit activities by staging fights.

"The gladiators used to draw real blood, too." Gallant observed. "But it was still only a circus.

"Assuming this was, too," he pursued the thought, "the most likely reason for it is that there is something in the library they don't want us to see."

"Is? You mean was. They've probably covered up by now if there was anything going on. We're a couple of prize dodos."

"Classic suckers. No one can resist running to a fight or a fire. They're the best stunts that exist. Well, let's go have a look anyway."

He jumped down off the stage.

"It's a good time if you want to search the place," Delamare told him. "The library's about to close down for the day. We can go through it without any bother."

Prisoner librarian Kapitänleutnant Siegfred Kuhn rose from his desk to meet the two visitors.

"Good afternoon," he said reservedly, standing by for them to make known their business. He sought to give his domain that hallowed air common to libraries and hospitals of a sanctum which must not be disturbed.

"Carry on," Gallant got rid of him, "we won't need you."

A quick glance around the main room sufficed to see that there were few places of concealment. The bookcases were bare metal shelving without backs. They stood row upon row filling two-thirds of the room but not touching the walls. Three large library tables without drawers and comfortable wooden armchairs made up the furnishings of the room. Several men were reading or making notes. The only possible places of concealment were the librarian's desk, the filing cabinet holding the card catalogue, and the books themselves.

A smaller adjoining room was devoted to periodicals. One of the two tables in the room had on it the latest issues of the usual popular magazines. At the other, three prisoners sat reading. On shelves similar to those in the main room were stacks of magazines.

"Closing time," Kuhn announced in a dignified but penetrating tone.

The men at the tables closed their books and got up to leave. Gallant and Delamare strolled back into the main room.

"We are closing now," Kuhn said again for their benefit.

"That's quite all right, just go along," Gallant told him as he slid open a drawer of the filing cabinet.

Kuhn waited at the door until the last man had left, then walked out himself, closing the door behind him. Gallant opened the other drawers, peering inside the cabinet to check on false bottoms or other hiding places. There were none. He gave the desk a quick going over then stood up to survey the room once more.

"Do you know if these books have been examined recently?" he asked Delamare.

"You mean, to see if they've been hollowed out or things like that? Not that I know of. In fact, I'm sure they haven't."

"Well," Gallant sighed, "we'll have to do it then. God damn bore."

"I can get some men to help us. Otherwise we'll be half the night."

"Go to it."

While waiting for Delamare to return with help, Gallant browsed through the shelves. The library contained a balanced selection of fiction and nonfiction, mainly in German, but nothing, as far as he could see, in the way of Nazi propaganda.

With the assistance of Delamare and a six-man squad, two of whom he assigned to the periodical room, Gallant ransacked the library, turning out every piece of reading material and sounding the walls and flooring. Covered with dust for their pains, the little group assembled at the librarian's desk, brushing their clothes as they awaited dismissal.

"First time I've ever been in a library without learning anything," Gallant quipped. "Maybe we'll have to try reading the books next time around."

"Gee, Captain," complained one of the men assigned to the periodical room, "you'd better get yourself another man. I wouldn't be able to make head or tail out of that technical stuff they have in there."

"Technical stuff? What kind?"

"Oh, all kinds. Real scientific."

"That so? We won't make you read it then. You men may go along now. Thank you."

"Let's have a look in there," Gallant said, heading toward the adjoining room after their assistants had left.

Ignoring the current magazines on the table, Gallant viewed the shelves where periodicals were piled in neat stacks. Curiously, there were no title names on the shelf edges as is customary in periodical rooms. He pulled out a magazine at random. *Petroleum News.* The next shelf down yielded *Motor Mechanics.* Samplings from other cases turned up *Engineering Digest, Aviation Weekly, Chemistry.*

Systematically, he moved from shelf to shelf, looking at the titles of all the periodicals. Without exception they were technical reviews. As far as he could judge, the room contained nearly all the scientific journals published in the United States and Canada.

"How the hell did they get their hands on all these, Del?" Gallant exploded. "Do you know what they could do with these?"

"I'm getting a vague idea—but it sounds farfetched."

"Not so farfetched, let me tell you," Gallant replied grimly. "This room contains the cornerstone of an espionage service.

All these publications are unavailable to Berlin since the war. They may get hold of some in neutral countries, but certainly not the whole collection that's here.

"Espionage isn't all cloak-and-dagger work. Most of it is done behind a desk by unspectacular types who know how to put two and two together. There probably isn't any one thing in these magazines that wouldn't get by censorship. In general, the editors know what they are doing. But if you put all these bits and pieces of information together, you can come up with something. A story on the production rate of one basic commodity can be a clue to our industrial capacity in a score of critical fields. Experts in various fields could have a heyday with these publications. And there are experts here, on almost any subject you can mention.

"I don't think they'd have much difficulty in getting the information out, either. They have ways. Or don't you agree?" he added, seeing Delamare frown.

"Oh, I know it all right. I was just thinking about the old man. He's going to hit the ceiling. This library is his pet project. He used to be in education, you know. I sort of suspect he might have given the okay for these magazines himself."

"So do I. Incredible! Well, I might as well find out."

"Now? It's after ten. You'll wake him. He'll get one of his ulcer attacks and won't be able to see straight. I'd let it go till tomorrow morning. After he's had breakfast."

"I suppose it can wait." Gallant accepted the advice. "But this place had better be closed down as of right now. Kuhn'll probably try to get in here first thing in the morning to wind up any unfinished business. I'll have the duty officer see to it."

"They're leaving the compound now, sir," the officer on watch in the dark at the front window of Barrack I reported to Modersohn, who was lying fully clothed on his bed.

"Stay at your post another fifteen minutes," Modersohn said in an undertone. "If they don't return, you may go to sleep."

Modersohn was not going to be caught unprepared if Gallant's inspection of the library resulted in a surprise inquisition. He stared into the darkness trying to outguess the enemy. That the afternoon's ruse had failed to divert Gallant from the library didn't necessarily mean he had tumbled to the use of the periodical room. It was a good sign that there hadn't been immediate repercussions. Perhaps Gallant wasn't as sharp as Kuhn's evaluation estimated. Kuhn was a thoroughgoing researcher but tended to be cautious in drawing conclusions. It was for these qualities that Modersohn had chosen Kuhn as his deputy in charge of espionage. Better to err on the side of safety than to go overboard.

Even if it were written off at this point, Modersohn consoled himself, the espionage group had served its purpose and could only be counted on the credit side of the ledger for him. Modersohn had formed the group shortly after his arrival at Bowmanville. In a few months, it had developed so successfully that Berlin had given it the status of a full-fledged organization. It was named the Lorient Group after the submarine base from which Modersohn had operated.

The Lorient Group had made two major contributions to the archives of Nazi intelligence. It had searched out a complete list of the locations of the major defense installations and production centers on the North American continent. The list was intended for sabotage purposes or bombing raids.

Second to this—but more important for immediate purposes —the Lorient Group kept up a steady flow of information on industrial capacity in America and occasionally on troop movements and training.

Modersohn thought with satisfaction of the mass of information Hans Zillich would be taking back to Germany shortly as an exchange prisoner. Coded letters were adequate and indicated for short, urgent messages, but exchange prisoners could handle lengthier reports and made more of an impression on Berlin.

Zillich was to be repatriated on the next neutral ship available. After intensive coaching by the two doctors among the prisoners, Zillich had managed to convince a medical board that he was suffering from permanent brain damage resulting from a concussion. It was amusing. Zillich mentally incapacitated! Zillich had memorized pages and pages of material to report to intelligence in Berlin.

CHAPTER 8

"Captain Gallant, you should have referred this matter to me last night," Colonel Perry said haughtily, his morning coffee stimulating his self-esteem. "For your information, I personally approved the librarian's request for scientific literature. I had an excellent reason for so doing."

"I'm sure you did, Colonel, but . . ."

"As I was saying, this was my decision, and I find you have overstepped your authority in ordering the library closed. You are overzealous and are conjuring up plots and see harm in innocuous situations."

"Colonel, if . . ."

Perry held up a thin, imperious hand.

"May I finish, please? You acted on paper-thin presumption. As a newspaperman"—Perry used the word as though it were dirty—"you tend, no doubt, to see the sensational in everything. There is absolutely no basis for concluding that these men are using the library material for the purpose of espionage. The notion is even more ludicrous if one considers the impossibility of transmitting any of this information.

"You amateurs," he said, "have little appreciation of what is involved here. I am not running an old-fashioned penal institution. I have a responsibility toward the future. The men in my charge need education—or reeducation—if they are to be of value in this world after the war. I'm giving them a chance to study new professions or to keep up with their old ones. It is commendable that they asked for scientific literature. You usurped authority in ordering the library closed," he repeated.

Perry rang a buzzer as he spoke. The corporal in the front office appeared in response.

"Corporal, have the library opened immediately."

"Yes, sir," the corporal answered.

"Colonel," Gallant attempted to reason with him, "I had no intention of usurping your authority. I took the initiative as I might have on the battlefield. It was the only logical move. I wish you would reconsider your counterorder. Even if my suspicions prove unfounded, the precaution is justifiable."

"They *are* unfounded, Captain Gallant."

Gallant decided to have another try. He lit a cigarette before continuing. The ashtray wasn't offered and he once again resorted to the wastepaper basket.

"Colonel, as you observed, I'm a newspaperman. But I'm not a sensation monger, and I'm not a brass check, either. As a newspaperman, I wrote what I thought was correct, and as a soldier, I act as I think proper.

"You say my action was improper, that my suspicions are unfounded. They are not unfounded; they are unproved. It's possible I may never get the proof, but that won't show that you are correct, either. It seems to me that the only course to take is to avert all possible risks."

"I completely agree," sniffed Perry. "We shall eliminate the entire risk and transfer Captain Modersohn forthwith as I originally wanted to do."

"And leave someone else to carry on with whatever he has initiated."

Gallant ground out his cigarette on the inside of the trash basket and rose to his feet.

"Sorry to have stepped on your toes in this library business—and I know I'm doing so again in mentioning it to you—but this is no time to worry about sensibilities. I'll have to insist that you keep Modersohn here."

Perry rose, removing the pince-nez from his quivering face. The offense to his pride was too great to bear.

"Captain Gallant," his voice squeaked, "I shall request your immediate recall and suggest disciplinary action on the basis of your insubordination. In the meantime, you will refrain from any activity whatsoever in this camp."

Gallant had his own particular theory of education for irrational adults: the shock treatment.

"Perry," he said calmly, "don't make an ass of yourself. I'm here to work with you, not for you. You'll discover that, much to your embarrassment, if you don't use the brain you're endowed with to better purpose.

"Your rank doesn't impress me one bit. It so happens that I'm fortunate enough to be able to go over your head. But I believe I'd act the same way even if I couldn't. At a certain point—a point that has to be decided by the individual—one has to follow the dictates of one's intellect, not of one's superior.

"I can see by your expression you think I'm seditious. Yet if I made my point another way, you'd undoubtedly agree with me.

"If I were a German and had the insight and the courage to disobey my government, you'd find that commendable, even heroic. A bit of a double standard, isn't it?

"You've been teaching obedience all your life. What if we had a Hitler here in Canada? Following your teachings, we'd be obeying him. Perhaps you should start thinking about a course in revolt as well. A class in comparative values. When to obey and when to revolt. How to think for yourself."

Gallant walked out, leaving Perry to his own counsel.

Perry's reopening of the library had one felicitous result. It brought confusion as well as comfort to the enemy.

A half hour after being informed that the library had been closed without explanation by Captain Gallant, Modersohn learned that it had been reopened on orders from Colonel Perry. On receipt of the first notice, Modersohn had immediately started writing a coded letter addressed to the sweetheart of Oberleutnant Rednitz, a mail drop for Intelligence. The letter was to inform Intelligence Chief Admiral Canaris that the Lorient Group would be out of operation until a new *modus operandi* could be found.

On receipt of the second notice, Modersohn destroyed the letter and drafted a new one. He informed Canaris that the Lorient Group was in a state of alert and that intensive work would be undertaken, disregarding precautions, to collate information in the latest periodicals and forward it posthaste. Modersohn then gave orders for the latest periodicals, including some which were due to arrive in that day's mail, to be taken from the library and analyzed in the barracks without interruption.

Not knowing if Perry would emerge from his state of shock still vindictive and actually bar him from the camp facilities, Gallant took possession of a jeep and drove into Bowmanville. Installing himself in the solitary telephone booth in the fusty lobby of the Lake Hotel, he placed a call to Ottawa. Soon he heard Kerr's familiar greeting:

"Gallant, what've you got?"

"I've got an old mother hen sitting on a hornet's nest insisting there's just an innocent little chick in there. I'm referring to the party who used to hatch out little Canadians. And I'm not being cute. I'm in a pay booth in a hotel in Bowmanville and there's a poster opposite me that says 'Even the walls have ears.'"

"Okay, that's twenty-five lines of local color. What else have you got?"

In a jargon comprehensible only to Kerr, Gallant explained the situation.

"What do you want me to do about it?" Kerr asked. "Get the old hen sent out to scratch in another backyard and close down the hall of learning?"

"Neither. What's done's done. I want the status quo but with cooperation. Any changes would sound the alarm. I think the man from the briny deep is a cautious soul.

"Have a heart-to-heart talk with the old boy and get him to play the game. If you can keep him friendly, fine. He's a well-meaning old bastard. He might still learn."

"I'll get onto him right away," Kerr promised. "What's your number there? I'll call you back."

A bellboy almost as ancient as the hotel summoned Gallant to the phone from the hotel dining room, where his regard for his fellowman had been restored by a chef who prepared an unexpectedly palatable lunch.

"All fixed," Kerr announced. "The old bastard wasn't too bad at all. Your lecture must have penetrated part way at least. I patted him on the head and I think he'll be fairly amenable from now on. You'll have to expect some squawks if things get risky, though."

"I know. He's afraid he's going to be pulled off the throne, by us if not by them.

"What's happening to Schröder?"

"Don't worry about him. We're making him our star boarder here. We checked him out on some technical stuff that we knew already and got straight answers. He's been in storage too long to have anything for us along those lines, but we did get a few new geographical details from him that we'll corroborate."

The geographical details, Gallant realized, would mean targets; the corroboration, a flight of Mosquito bombers.

The three German officers strolling along the side road leading to the camp moved to one side to allow Gallant's jeep to pass. They were out on parole, he knew. Every day a group of officers was allowed to leave the compound to walk through the neighboring countryside.

Without exception, the prisoners were very proud of the fact that their parole was never broken. Gallant had heard over and over again that the officers boasted that no one had ever tried to escape while out on parole. They made much of this proof of their honor as though it established their respectability in general.

Honor was not involved, Gallant knew. Only constraint. Any man who broke parole would face devastating reprisals for the rest of his life. The momentary sensation of liberty fostered by the walks was too precious to sacrifice. And one violation would mean the end of that liberty for everyone.

The three U-boat officers Gallant passed were observing the meaning of their parole in the precise sense only. They were not escaping, but they were engaged in other activity which was not aboveboard.

"The big pine there." Oberleutnant Felix Krafft pointed. "We could put a rock under it."

"Too close to the road," objected Kapitänleutnant Julius Schmidt. "We could be seen."

The third officer, Oberleutnant Christian Hochbauer, surveyed the terrain with a practiced eye.

"That won't do," he said. "I want someplace even closer to the road. Someplace I can get to fast without creating suspicion by roaming all over the woods. How about the other side? The forest is nearer to the road there."

Crossing the road they walked along the shoulder. Under a telephone pole Krafft picked up a short length of wire that a linesman had discarded. He wound it carefully around his waist underneath his trouser band. The officers on promenade were assiduous junk collectors.

"Here," Hochbauer said, seating himself on a fallen tree lying on the shoulder parallel to the road. "You could sit here looking natural and I could stop and pretend to be making a repair in case someone comes along."

His hand explored in back of the log.

"Look, just what we want. A hollow spot underneath. See?"

"Good," Schmidt approved. "Let's all take a bearing on this spot. Twenty meters from the big pine in that direction"—he pointed toward the camp—"and thirty, no thirty-five meters from the bend in the road that way. You could find it in the dark if you had to."

"I could find it with my eyes closed," Hochbauer boasted. "I'll be able to smell it out if the money is there."

"Don't count on it," Schmidt rebuked him. "The money may never come. It should have arrived last week at the latest."

"Maybe it will come today and we won't have to come back for it."

"Maybe, maybe. Better we count on getting along without it. We have the alternate plan."

By tacit agreement, Perry and Gallant bypassed excuses and explanations on the latter's return and entered immediately into discussion of the means to thwart the presumed espionage.

"I imagine," Gallant began diplomatically, "we've somewhat confused our friends in the compound. With any luck, we can keep them that way for a while. Or at least try to.

"We can take it for granted whatever is in the library now has been used and is water over the dam. We might as well leave it open and just see to it that they don't get any more material. They'll suspect what's happening, but they'll also have to take into consideration the possibility of a delay in the mail. Maybe we can keep them guessing for a while. I don't really have high hopes of fooling them, but it won't cost us anything and perhaps we can learn something about their operation if they don't cover up right away."

Perry nodded his approval.

"Do you know, by the way," Gallant continued, "if any periodicals came in today?"

"I can find out easily enough," the colonel answered, picking up the telephone and repeating the request to a clerk in the censorship room.

"Yes sir, five," he was told after the records were consulted.

"Five," Perry repeated guiltily.

He looked at the onyx clock on his desk.

"Perhaps it isn't too late to recover them." He picked up the phone again and asked to be connected with the tower guards at the entrance to the compound.

"Is mail call still on?" he inquired of the soldiers.

The guard looked down at the parade ground. The group around the corporal distributing the mail was breaking up. Among those walking away was the librarian, Kapitänleutnant Kuhn. He carried two packages. Bunched in one were the magazines. The other contained ten books, classics to which no one could object. They had been opened and inspected by censorship.

"Mail call is just over, sir," the guard reported.

Dropping the phone back in place, Perry shook his head negatively at Gallant.

"Oh, a few more or less at this point," Gallant consoled him. He reached into his pocket for a cigarette. Perry brought out the VIP ashtray.

"As we stand now," Gallant began outlining his plans, "there's no positive action open to us. We can only observe and probe."

To allay the colonel's apprehensions, he amended: "That's not as bad as it sounds. So far we've done rather well. Schröder revealed some important information, and at the very least we did uncover a breach of security in the library. We could crack down on them right now, but it's to our advantage to learn more."

The colonel continued his nervous little nods of agreement.

"In the probing department," Gallant said thoughtfully, "I'd like to see if we could turn up another person like Schröder. Do you know of any element that's in discord with Modersohn or the others? Has the Ältestenrat had anyone up on charges?"

"No, we haven't heard anything. Schröder was the only case and, as you know, that came into the open by pure accident."

"Hmm," Gallant reflected. "What's your censorship staff like?" Fairly alert bunch? What I'm driving at is that, if they're capable of reading in between the lines, they may spot signs of discontent in someone. It might come in the form of a vague impression they wouldn't ordinarily notice. Perhaps there's someone who avoids writing anything about politics or patriotism, who doesn't use the stock jingoistic expressions."

"I'm afraid that would be beyond this censorship staff, Captain. They're of average intelligence but no more. They were selected strictly for their knowledge of German, which they got by birth, not application. They are all of German extraction. The headquarters staffs cornered the cream of the crop. We got what was left. We haven't a large German-speaking population in Canada."

"Well, I'll sit in with them then and give it a whirl by myself. It's a long shot, particularly for one man, but I'll give it all the time I can until something else pops up.

"The other leads we can follow stem from the espionage setup. They have two obvious means of transmission. One is by code or disappearing ink. Kerr is arranging for that. The cypher experts in his department will have a look-see at the mail. About all they can do is to spot-check it, though, in the hope that they'll tumble on something. The difficulty lies in finding code, not in cracking it. I'm told there's no code that can't be broken—given enough time.

"The other obvious method of transmission is via a man who is being repatriated."

"Oh?" Perry reacted.

"You have one?"

"Yes," Perry said uncertainly, "but I hardly think he'd be capable. A medical board certified him mentally incapacitated. He suffered a severe concussion."

"Let's have a chat with Major Farnsworth," Gallant proposed.

The chat with Major Farnsworth elicited what Gallant suspected, medicine not being an exact science. Based on the medical evidence and on precedent, the diagnosis of Farnsworth and the board was justified. There did exist though, Farnsworth readily admitted, an infinitesimal possibility—perhaps one-tenth of one percent—that Zillich was malingering. In such cases the patient was given the benefit of the doubt.

"Except," as Gallant pointed out, "when an espionage ring is in question."

Colonel Perry did not demur.

"Can you put a stop order on him?" Gallant asked Kerr. "Wait till he gets out of Bowmanville and hold him someplace else?"

"I can, but it might involve us in reprisals and complications with the Swiss. These exchanges are on a *quid pro quo* basis. One of our boys will get held out if Zillich doesn't go."

"Send a substitute. There must be a waiting list. You can say Zillich is too ill to be moved."

Kerr's cough rumbled across the line. Gallant removed the phone from his ear.

"Swiss won't like it," he heard as he replaced the receiver. "Have to lie to them. And the Germans won't believe it. They've probably been tipped off in code that he's carrying information."

"So we let him go?"

"No," Kerr said bitterly. "I'll run in a ringer and let the Swiss fight it out with the Germans, *À la guerre comme à la guerre.*"

"I know, old man," Gallant answered softly, the decision weighing heavily on him as well.

On the way to the library, Kuhn had stopped briefly at Barrack VII, where he bunked. When he left the barrack, he was no longer carrying the periodicals and his other package was two books lighter. The periodicals were whisked over to Barrack V under the jacket of a fledgling leutnant. There they were taken in charge by an oberleutnant who immediately got to work analyzing them. Two other officers, one inside, one outside, stood watch.

A similar watch was being maintained over Barrack VII, where a luftwaffe officer was operating on the two classics. Like many youths of the post-World War I era in Germany, the officer had been a glider enthusiast. He had even constructed his own craft out of canvas glued onto wooden frames. Forbidden powered aircraft by the Versailles Treaty, Germany had stimulated this glider activity to maintain a foot in the door.

With the painstaking skill he had learned in airframe construction, the luftwaffe man dampened and pulled back, without damaging it, the heavy paper on the inside of each of the four covers. In the center of each was a precision-cut rectangle in which were compressed fifteen twenty-dollar bills. While a fellow officer carried the money to Barrack I, where Modersohn awaited it, the luftwaffe man fitted new cardboard into the covers and reglued the job as skillfully as it had been done in the bindery.

"Exactly twelve hundred dollars, sir," the officer reported, putting the money on the table in front of Modersohn. The fregattenkapitän acknowledged him with the barest of nods. The man saluted and left rapidly.

"Tell Schmidt and Hochbauer," Modersohn ordered von Sperle, "and code a letter to Admiral Doenitz confirming receipt of this and that we are on schedule."

Picking up the money, he left the barrack and marched across the parade ground to Barrack III, where, for safekeeping overnight, he stored it in the tunnel entrance. Surprise inspections were infrequent in Bowmanville and the last one had been held recently. But Modersohn was taking no chances. The tunnel was the most secure hiding place in camp.

To avoid calling attention to Barrack III, Modersohn visited it with no more frequency than he did the others. He profited by his unplanned visit to inspect the shaft, more for reasons of morale than anything else. Von Sperle and Unger alternately furnished him with daily progress reports, the competition effectively insuring that both men stayed on their toes. But it did the working crews good to see their commanding officer appear unexpectedly in the dirty, uncomfortable tunnel. Schooled though they were in obedience, Modersohn knew there existed a minority who obeyed only reluctantly.

The letter von Sperle had prepared for Doenitz was completed and ready for Modersohn's inspection by the time he arrived back at Barrack I. It was addressed to von Sperle's mother, who would communicate it to the admiral. The code was not the same as that used in letters to Intelligence. It was a less sophisticated variety selected by the individualistic Doenitz without recourse to Intelligence's cipher section.

"Good." Modersohn handed the letter back to von Sperle. "There is time for it to catch this afternoon's post."

Beginning in the late afternoon, following his call to Kerr, and continuing into the evening after the staff had left, Gallant sat in the bleak censorship room doggedly sampling letter after letter. Several hours of browsing confirmed what he already knew: most people write horribly dull, banal letters. More to the point, in not one of them had he come across any sign of disenchantment with the Nazis.

Having known at the outset that it was a plodding, probably hopeless undertaking, Gallant controlled the feeling of futility that surged up from time to time.

Shortly after eight, Delamare came silently into the office to "see how things were going."

"Still got all those to do." Gallant indicated two sacks of mail. "Don't suppose I'll get around to all of them."

"Well, I'm on duty tonight if you need anything," Delamare volunteered.

"Wouldn't be any coffee around?"

"I might even get you a sandwich," Delamare answered, sensing that Gallant hadn't taken time out for dinner. "I think they're still cleaning up in the mess hall."

While waiting for Delamare to return, Gallant opened one of the mail sacks. He skimmed through a number of letters, eventually coming to the one written that afternoon by von Sperle. Interested because he knew him to be Modersohn's aide, Gallant looked at the letter more attentively. He gave it a complete reading and found it slightly more literate than the run of the mill but hardly more interesting. Glancing at it a second time to analyze the handwriting, a practice he was given to, Gallant noticed a peculiarity in the date heading the sheet. It was written in Roman numerals, not unheard of but sufficiently out of the ordinary to call for further study. Gallant couldn't recall the use of Roman numerals in any of the other letters.

When Delamare returned, he found Gallant rapidly opening and refolding letters, checking to see if there were any other instances of that form.

"Can you get me some men to go through the rest of these two sacks, Del?" he asked. "They don't have to read German. All they have to do is see if the date is written like this," he said, explaining why.

While the sergeant and five men he had rounded up opened and closed letters, Gallant placed a call to Kerr at home, and described the letter to him.

"There's nothing much we can do about it tonight. They keep banker's hours here," Kerr commented. "Send it up by special messenger and I'll have it given the full treatment first thing in the morning."

Perfunctorily eating his sandwich and sipping the lukewarm coffee, Gallant went back to scanning the letters that remained. No other examples of the Roman-numeral date turned up.

CHAPTER 9 The letter was waiting for Kerr when he arrived in his office at 8 A.M. He summoned a cipher expert, who came from an adjoining building within five minutes. The expert was a young man who approached his job with the air of a medical diagnostician. Picking up the letter, he gave it a general once-over, emitted a few nasal sounds which could not be interpreted as either positive or negative.

"See anything there or do you have a catarrh?" Kerr asked, his neutral tone making it difficult to determine if he was being humorous or annoyed.

"If it's what I think it is, it's rather ridiculous," the cipher man pronounced, too preoccupied to take offense. "Since there's a rush about this, perhaps you'd like me to call in our section chief for consultation. He'll know immediately if my suspicions are correct."

Kerr handed him the phone. The cipher man put through the connection.

"Devereux? Can you come over here? I'm in the brigadier's office. I think we have something in the way of an antique that would interest you. Rather amazing but I'm almost positive we have an example here of Code Irland."

Devereux's reply brought a look of amusement to his junior's face.

"Yes, I know," he answered. "That's what surprised me. I thought we'd save some time if you had a look at it. I knew you'd seen it."

"What is Code Irland?" Kerr asked as the cipher man replaced the receiver.

"It was a World War I German naval code. Some chap in England cracked it, in 1915 I believe it was. Don't know exactly how it works, but Devereux will. I just recall hearing it used Roman numerals."

The door opened and an elderly man entered.

"Oh, Devereux," the young expert said eagerly, "here, look at this."

Devereux greeted Kerr and settled a pair of reading glasses on his nose before taking the letter.

"Hmm . . . yes, yes," he murmured, "it looks like Irland . . . unless by coincidence the writer is genuinely using Roman numerals to indicate the date. Last time I saw this was in 1916, if memory serves me. Makes us both rather relics, doesn't it?

"I suppose the Germans never did learn that we cracked it. But still, the idea of using a World War I code! Strikes me as rather amateurish. We'll see what it's all about for you, but I shouldn't expect it's anything of importance. Probably just a personal note written by an officer who knew the old code. If it were important, they'd surely use something recent that's a bit harder to detect."

"Run it through for me anyway as fast as you can, will you please, Devereux?" Kerr asked.

"Surely, surely. Have it done in no time at all. It's a simple code, really. The Roman numerals serve two purposes. When the reader sees them, he knows the letter is in code. Then, the date itself serves as the key. It indicates at what point the alphabet is split up into dots and dashes. The rest is straight Morse, with the first letter of each word forming the message. Child's play, no?"

Kerr raised an eyebrow.

"Not quite. There are a couple of points I don't follow, but never mind. I'll take your word for it."

"I can explain," the cipher chief offered.

Kerr held up his hand.

"Just give me the results." He smiled.

As they left the office, Kerr shouted through the open door for Miss Griffon to get Bowmanville on the line.

"You've got a nibble," he informed Gallant, explaining the circumstances.

"I don't see von Sperle writing to the old mater in archaic code," Gallant opined. "He's not the type, not old enough either to know a code from the first world war."

"No, it's not in character," Kerr agreed. "But there must be a reason for it. Maybe we'll find out when we get the transcript. Meanwhile, chew on it. It's an intriguing sort of detail."

Gallant found the detail intriguing, too. Before secluding himself to "chew on it," he stopped at the censorship room to tell the crew there to be on the lookout for letters employing

Roman numerals. He also asked if they had ever noticed the numerals before. The reply was an uncertain no.

His feet propped on his desk, eyes closed, Gallant meditated. When, fifty minutes later, Kerr called back, he had formed an incomplete theory.

"It was Irland," Kerr said in his succinct manner. "Here's the message: 'One thousand two hundred received. Kiebitz on schedule.' Mean anything to you?"

"Not a thing."

"I was thinking 'Kiebitz' might be the name of an agent or the code name for an operation."

"Sounds logical. How about the number? Doesn't sound like the number of an agent. And you don't usually refer to an agent as being 'received.' You'd say 'arrived' or 'contacted' or something like that. My guess is that it's something they actually received, probably hidden in a package."

"That's the way I figure it, too. I had another idea but I already checked that out. I thought it might refer to the number of a radio message. There are sets concealed in most of the camps. Somehow, they manage to construct them. We monitor almost everything, though, and that number doesn't correspond to any message we've heard. Also, even if they do have a shortwave set, it's unlikely to be powerful enough so that they'd rely on it for messages."

"So that brings us back to something smuggled in—twelve hundred somethings. They'd have to be small. Offhand I can only think of one thing they might want twelve hundred of."

"Yes, and they wouldn't have to be in single dollar bills. In big denominations they wouldn't be hard to conceal."

"Unfortunately," Gallant answered. "They would be damn easy to hide here, too. I doubt if a search would uncover them. Do I make one, or do we continue to stand pat?"

"It's your show. What do you want to do?"

"That depends on what we do with the letter. Do we send it on or not?"

"Still your show."

"Let me think it over. I'll get back to you later, after I speak to Perry."

"Right."

"Oh, one other thing," Gallant said hastily, before Kerr hung up. "I was muddling over the use of Code Irland. My guess is that von Sperle wrote the letter by proxy for Modersohn. But it doesn't seem like the sort of code Modersohn would use, either. He didn't serve in World War I."

"But do you remember what Schröder said about Modersohn, that he's Doenitz's favorite? Doenitz served in the first war and he could have had access to a naval code. The hitch is that it's not logical for him to be using it now."

"Don't worry about the logic. The fact is, it is being used," Kerr said. "Your theory's not bad. It might help fill in the picture somewhere along the line."

Walking down the corridor to Perry's office, Gallant tried to calculate the use Modersohn might intend for the money, if money it was. He dismissed all peaceful uses. The POWs lacked nothing in Bowmanville. For espionage? Not very likely unless Modersohn was employing agents outside the camp and that was improbable. No, the most logical assumption was that Modersohn would follow his previous pattern: a sabotage attempt by escaped prisoners. Money would be needed both for living expenses and for the purchase of equipment.

Perry listened to the new development with determined calm. He even placed the ashtray on his desk before Gallant started smoking. Only the twitch which pinched his nostrils indicated his perturbation.

"This is what you've been waiting for, I suppose," he said.

"Now you know what they're planning. We're free at last to take countermeasures."

"We don't know by a long shot what they're planning," Gallant corrected. "We're merely sure that they're planning something and we've made a wild guess about what it might be. Even so, I think it might be wise to crack down on them before things get out of hand."

Perry looked much relieved and Gallant continued: "Our first step should be to prevent a break. As I understand it, a surprise inspection for disguises and tools is the most effective precautionary measure."

"Ordinarily, yes," Perry answered, his troubled demeanor returning. "However, I fear that an inspection would be fruitless at this moment. I had a very thorough search made of the entire compound after the riot, the day before you arrived here, to be exact. Not one solitary object was discovered, which is unheard of. I can only conclude that they have a hiding place which escapes our detection. And I assure you we've made every effort to uncover it."

"I don't doubt that you have, Colonel," Gallant sympathized. "There's definitely no use our looking for whatever it was that was mentioned in the letter. We'd have to literally tear the whole camp apart to find anything small enough to have come by mail—reduce all the buildings to rubble, dig up the entire compound and stick our fingers you know where."

"What can we do then, Captain?" Perry questioned humbly.

"Play the game out. Send the letter on to von Sperle's mother and double our vigilance here. Could you have the officers and noncoms make extra rounds and deliver a talk to the men, jack them up a bit?"

"By all means. I was going to speak to the men anyway, as a matter of routine. Half the troops are being rotated tonight. We do that every three months in all the camps. Keeps the men on their toes not to stay too long in one camp. It also obviates the possibility of the prisoners' exploiting any familiarity with the guards."

"Isn't it difficult to break in new men all the time?" Gallant wanted to know.

"They are not precisely new. The work is about the same in all the camps. And we do maintain a permanent cadre of supervisory and office personnel."

CHAPTER 10 At seven o'clock that evening a convoy of trucks carrying the new guards rolled past the compound gate on its way to the troop quarters. A prisoner stationed opposite the gate confirmed their arrival to von Sperle.

The same trucks left an hour later taking with them the contingent of men being replaced. The new arrivals settled into the bunks vacated by the old troops and then went to the mess hall for a late dinner. Being older men, fatigued by the day's trip, most of them retired early, immediately after a pep talk by Colonel Perry, to which they listened with the customary inattention. The new troops were not to go on duty that night and few of them even saw the rest of the camp's contingent.

At nine the following morning a platoon of the new troops

took over the guard posts. They settled into the routine easily, having done similar work in the other POW camps spread across Canada. Only the faces of the prisoners and of the men they relieved were different.

Shortly after nine o'clock two men wearing the uniform of privates in the Veterans' Guard crossed the section of the compound in back of the recreation hall carrying a ladder, a bucket of cement, and two trowels. The four guards in the towers commanding that section of the yard saw nothing unusual in their presence there. Maintenance work was a regular occurrence in all the camps.

The two privates crossed the trip wire without hesitation and walked up to a point in the wall indicated by one of them. They looked at it critically, then placed the ladder against the wall.

One of the two guards in the tower near where they were laying out their equipment craned his neck to see what they were going to repair. He noticed a crack in the bricks running to the top of the wall. Meanwhile, one of the men was stirring the cement; the other was running a trowel along the crack, cleaning out the loose matter.

Starting at the bottom of the wall, the pair unhurriedly cemented the crack, working upward. From time to time one of the guards glanced their way. When they reached shoulder height, one of the men climbed a few rungs up the ladder and continued troweling. The other followed him, holding the bucket. So, in tandem, they reached the top of the wall, where they paused for a break, lighting up cigarettes.

Seated on the wall they smoked for a minute, chatting, and then started cleaning a break in the top of the wall, brushing the debris over the side. One of the men looked over the outer side and said something to his partner. The latter looked over, too, lay down on the top, and leaned over the edge to dig at the wall with his trowel, dislodging some loose concrete.

Standing up, the pair hauled the ladder hand over hand to the top of the wall and let it down again on the outer side. Then, reversing the process, they cleaned and cemented the crack from top to bottom. Only occasionally did one of the guards satisfy his curiosity and look at them. For the most part the guards kept their eyes on the prisoners within the compound.

When the two soldiers completed their job, they picked up the ladder and walked parallel to the wall to the nearest corner. Once around it, they cut across the fields to a dirt road leading to the prison farm. If any one of the new guards on that side of the wall noticed them, the sight presented nothing out of the way. They all had been briefed on the geography of the camp and knew that a farm worked by the prisoners on the honor system lay in that direction, hidden from sight by the woods. Despite the officers' being on parole, a token force of guards supervised the farm.

Without hurrying, the pair followed the road. Once out of sight in the wooded stretch, they quickened their pace and turned onto a path. Fifty yards in, hidden from the road, they slid the ladder and the rest of their equipment under a thick growth of bushes.

Walking at a swift pace now and keeping to the woods, they circled two sides of the farm. Then they headed in a direct line for Highway 2, about two miles distant at that point. Despite the uneven ground, they covered the distance in under twenty minutes. Within sight of the highway, they stopped in the shelter of some bushes to take off their uniforms and conceal them in the undergrowth. Underneath they wore civilian clothing. The Veterans' Guard uniforms on close inspection might have been detected as only reasonable facsimiles. They had been made by the prisoners' tailoring shop.

The clothing they now wore also had been made or converted by the tailoring shop, except that it was indistinguishable from garments which might be worn by the average Canadian civilian. Both wore cotton trousers of the type known as suntans. One had on a white shirt and a sleeveless gray sweater. The other sported a brown shirt and a black jersey sweater.

Kapitänleutnant Julius Schmidt and Oberleutnant Christian Hochbauer, respectively commanders of the late U-110 and U-122, also had new, faultless Canadian identities to go with their clothing.

In Schmidt's shirt pocket were papers identifying him as Walter Crowninshield, a twenty-six-year-old Canadian, honorably discharged from the navy for wounds suffered in combat. He had a scar on his chest to match the description. The papers, which included a driver's license, were extremely fine counterfeits, made in Germany. The six hundred Canadian dollars, however, which he carried in his trouser pocket were genuine, even though they, too, had come from Berlin.

Christian Hochbauer carried the other half of the twelve-hundred-dollar bankroll. His driver's license was made out in the name of Christian Foucauld, born in Quebec in 1919, and his draft card showed he had been deferred from military service for physical disability.

Both men spoke English faultlessly. If Hochbauer had the faintest of accents at times, it could be attributed to the French Canadian origin he had assumed. Until the age of fifteen Hochbauer had lived in Cairo, where his father worked as an engineer. In that cosmopolitan environment, he had learned and commonly used both English and French. Schmidt's father had served as German consul in both England and the United States. His primary and secondary school education had been in those countries.

Hochbauer and Schmidt stepped out of the woods onto the King's highway at five minutes to eleven according to the inexpensive but accurate wristwatch Schmidt wore. It was an American watch which had been obtained from one of the guards who had fancied a regulation luftwaffe chronometer.

"Ten minutes ahead of schedule," Schmidt noted with satisfaction. Every movement had been calculated and organized by the escape committee. Where possible, alternatives had been provided.

They were now to walk west at a normal pace for one mile, where they would come to a bus stop. The bus was due at 11:15. A new spring schedule had been printed in the *Oshawa Times* two months ago and had been noted and filed by the external intelligence service. The bus would stop, they had been informed, in response to a hand signal. It would carry them through Bowmanville, where it would make a scheduled stop, to Oshawa, eleven miles beyond. There, to throw off pursuit, they were to change for a train to Toronto.

En route to the bus stop, their instructions were to try to hitch a ride. Their objective was to get away from the immediate area of the prison camp as rapidly as possible. Theoretically, they were relatively safe once their masquerade carried them beyond the compound wall. The next roll call was not until evening. But there was always the possibility of a surprise check or of latent suspicions by one of the guards.

Few vehicles were on the road. Five minutes went by before they heard the hum of an engine behind them. Glancing back but continuing to walk, they stuck out their thumbs. A sedan with only a couple in it swept by them.

"Not so generous, these Canadians, after all," Schmidt sneered.

"Did you see that girl? I wouldn't have stopped either if I was with her."

Hochbauer's two years of celibacy weighed heavily on him. Try as he might to keep his thoughts on his mission, he couldn't avoid flights of fantasy concerning his first night of freedom. Schmidt tried to persuade himself he was made of sterner stuff. He flashed Hochbauer a look of annoyance.

A few more minutes of trudging and the square nose of a jeep topped the rise in front of them. Both noticed it immediately but kept on walking down the highway. Their impulse, already that of the hunted, was to break for the woods, but they had been instructed to carry on normally in such a situation. If there was an alarm out for them and they were spotted, there was little hope in flight. Better to brazen it out.

Hochbauer tried desperately to think of something to say to prove his aplomb to Schmidt.

"If they were going our way, maybe we could hitch a ride." He grinned.

Schmidt returned his tight smile.

"There are only two of them. If they stop us, we jump them."

"Okay. We'll have our own transportation."

The jeep slowed as it came abreast of them, but its passenger glanced at them without interest. The driver's attention was focused on a truck coming in the opposite direction.

Belatedly, Hochbauer signaled to the truck when it was almost upon them, neither he nor Schmidt having noticed it before. Airbrakes hissing, the truck pulled onto the shoulder of the road. Surprised, the two Germans didn't react until the truck came to a halt, then ran toward it.

"Going through to Toronto, if it's any help to you," the driver offered as Schmidt opened the door.

"Uh, thanks," Schmidt hesitated, tempted but fearing it would make them too easy to trace if they accepted a ride to their destination.

"Can you drop us at Oshawa? We're heading for Beaverton. I think we have to turn north from Oshawa, don't we?"

The cover story came easily to Schmidt. He had never expected to use it, so was grateful now for the hours of tedious memorization insisted upon by Modersohn.

"Beaverton?" The truck driver furrowed his brow. "Yeah, that's right. It's about forty miles straight north from Oshawa. Hop in."

The two men jumped into the spacious cab and the truck started on its way again, its driver content to have company on his lonely run. His passengers weren't too talkative, but he did learn that they were on their way to pick up a truck and had missed their bus. If he had been asked to describe them later, he would have said they were ordinary-looking guys, both had brown hair and were of medium height. As far as he was concerned, they were a couple of regular Joes. He was low on cigarettes and they weren't stingy about sharing theirs, even though they were hard to come by because of the war. He dropped them near the bus station in Oshawa.

Without asking directions, having memorized a street map of Oshawa, Schmidt and Hochbauer made their way to the vicinity of the railroad station. While Hochbauer went into a luncheonette opposite the station, Schmidt bought a round-trip ticket to Toronto. He then entered the luncheonette, choosing a seat several places away from Hochbauer. When the latter finished his lunch, he crossed to the station and bought a one-way ticket to Toronto. He spent the fifteen minutes to train time reading a newspaper in the waiting room. Hochbauer went directly from the restaurant to the station platform. Both men entered the same car but chose separate seats. Hochbauer also had picked up a newspaper and they both passed the short journey reading to avoid conversation with their seat partners.

In Toronto they left the station separately, on the lookout for signs of a dragnet. They rejoined each other three blocks away, confident that they were not yet the objects of a search.

Entering a popular low-priced department store crowded

with midday shoppers, each on his own to avoid later identification, Hochbauer and Schmidt purchased a few changes of
clothing, some toilet articles, and cheap valises. Hochbauer
used the store lavatory to place his packages in his valise and
don the poplin windbreaker he had bought. Schmidt accomplished the same task in a public lavatory nearby. He emerged
wearing an imitation leather jacket. They met by prearrange-
ment at the soda fountain of a drugstore on the corner.

The next step was to find lodgings. They were to avoid cheap
hotels and lodging houses, which were frequently kept under
surveillance by the police. Good hotels were out of the question, clothed as they were. Their instructions were to use the
classified ads to find a room with a private family. A bit of
natural curiosity on the part of a householder was preferable to
police supervision.

Underlining likely room-for-rent ads in the *Toronto Star*
while having a cup of coffee, Hochbauer and Schmidt felt full
of confidence. So far their escape had gone even better than
foreseen.

Carrying their suitcases, they left the drugstore and set about
following down the ads. By six o'clock, they had managed to
visit only four places, all of which were already rented. The
evening was no time to look for a room in a private household,
they had been warned, so they turned to the alternate solution:
the YMCA.

"No rooms," a desk clerk told them. "Lots of servicemen on
leave."

Obligingly, the clerk offered to store their cumbersome valises while they searched elsewhere, not that he held out much
hope for them.

Schmidt and Hochbauer stood on the sidewalk outside the
YMCA as much at a loss about where to go as two dateless
youths on a Saturday night.

"God damn it, we must find a place," Schmidt swore, mindful of their warning to avoid at all costs spending the night on the street, where they might be picked up by the police.

"Let's have dinner," the practical Hochbauer suggested, it being seven o'clock, one hour later than their accustomed mealtime at Bowmanville. "Everything closes early in this town and we'll have to go without eating if we wait much longer."

They walked down the street in the direction of some shops. Hochbauer looked around carefully to see if anyone was near them.

"Do you think we could find a German restaurant?" he whispered nostalgically.

"Don't be a fool."

They were to stay away from Germans. Only in case of emergency were they to contact a German resident of Toronto whose name they had been given and who was considered sympathetic to the Nazi cause.

"What I would give for some good home cooking," Hochbauer sighed.

Inside the steamy plate-glass window of one shop glowed a neon sign: "RESTAURANT." As they turned into its doorway, the smaller letters in the sign became visible: "KOSHER." Hochbauer pulled up short, started to draw back. Schmidt's fingers dug into his arm, holding him. Schmidt pretended to read the menu scotch-taped to the window.

"Act naturally, idiot."

Hochbauer stared at the menu.

"This is perfect. It's the last place anyone would think of looking for us," Schmidt whispered.

They entered the restaurant. Several people were dining, but no waitress was visible. They chose a table at the back of the room and sat facing forward. A bullet-headed elderly man emerged from the kitchen and, coming up behind them, placed two menus on the table.

"Gut eefeening," he said, his unmistakably German accent

startling them. He walked away, leaving them to consult the menu.

"He's a German," Hochbauer whispered behind his menu.

"He's a Jew," Schmidt differentiated, also shielding himself with the menu.

The bullet-headed man came back, a pencil and pad in his hands, and stood waiting for them to order. Uncomfortable, Hochbauer couldn't focus his attention on the menu and, when Schmidt gave his order, mumbled, "I'll have the same."

A waitress set their first course in front of them: pickled herring. They started eating. After the first bite, Hochbauer went at it enthusiastically.

"It's like German food," he said out of the corner of his mouth.

"He's a refugee," Schmidt said in explanation.

Hochbauer glanced at the old man, who had taken his place behind the cashier's desk. Their eyes met.

The waitress returned with their second course, a heaping plate of pot roast and dumplings. Alongside it she set a dish of coleslaw. They both dug in heartily.

"It is German food," Hochbauer insisted. He glanced at the cashier's desk again. The old man was looking at them. Hochbauer retreated to his food and ate rapidly.

"More dumplings?" the waitress offered.

They both accepted. The man at the desk watched as she piled the dumplings on their plates.

"He's watching us," Hochbauer said nervously, holding his napkin to his mouth. "He knows we're German. Jew or not, he's from Germany and he can recognize a German. Let's get out of here."

"Don't be an ass," Schmidt muttered. "Eat. Finish your meal. It'll attract attention otherwise."

They ate without further conversation, unmistakably under observation by the old man. Hastily they gulped their dessert, an apple strudel, and Schmidt called for the check. "PLEASE PAY THE CASHIER" was printed at the bottom of it.

Schmidt placed the check and a five-dollar bill on the rubber mat of the cashier's desk.

"Pardon me for staring at you," the restaurant man said, his accent and appearance shockingly Germanic to Schmidt and Hochbauer.

Here it comes, thought Hochbauer. *He's spotted us as Germans. When the alarm goes out, he'll remember and put them on our trail.*

"It does me good," the man continued, "to see young Canadian Jewish boys eating our food with such pleasure. Over here, usually it's only the older folks who like it."

Schmidt managed a smile, picked up his change.

"It was very good," he said.

Hochbauer added a weak smile to Schmidt's as they went out the door.

"He thought we were Jews," Hochbauer muttered wonderingly.

They walked rapidly down the street, eager to get away from the restaurant, and continued walking aimlessly until they came upon what looked like a modest but decent little hotel.

"It's not a palace," Schmidt judged, "but it's still the sort of place where they'd expect you to wear a suit and necktie."

"Let's go in anyway," Hochbauer urged. "It's less of a risk than roaming the streets all night."

Self-consciously, they entered the hotel.

"Full up," the desk clerk announced. "Try the YMCA. I don't think there's a free hotel room in the whole town."

Disoriented, they walked the streets again. A steeple clock boomed out nine o'clock. It was zero hour. Evening roll call was being held at Bowmanville. If their escape hadn't been detected yet, this was the critical moment.

CHAPTER 11

Under the floodlights of the guard towers, the prisoners formed up for evening roll call on the parade ground facing the gate. Each of the seven barracks formed a separate group, ten men abreast, making the formation easy to verify. The first three, smaller barracks, held eighty men apiece; the others, one hundred forty each. Bowmanville had a full complement.

The leader of each barrack stood in front of his group facing a noncommissioned officer of the camp staff. When the order was given over the loudspeaker, the barrack leader started the count-off in rotation. Each man sang out his number while the Canadian noncommissioned officer kept watch.

"Barrack I, count off!" blared Captain Howell over the loud-speaker.

Modersohn, commanding Barrack I, barked a crisp "One." "Two," echoed von Sperle. Each man in turn shouted his number until eighty was reached.

"Eighty, all present and accounted for," reported Modersohn.

"Barrack I, eighty, all present and accounted for!" the noncom bellowed his confirmation to Howell.

"Barrack II, count off!" ordered Howell.

Kapitänleutnant Franz Wallau, in charge of Barrack II, started the count. Schmidt was quartered in Barrack II, but despite his absence eighty voices responded to the count-off. Leutnant Heisler of Barrack IV was standing in for him. The noncom checking the count noted only that there were ten lines of eight men each, the individual faces meaning nothing to him. He heard eighty voices respond and confirmed the count as correct.

The corporal responsible for Barrack IV also checked his lines and saw that he had the required ten columns of fourteen men each. During the count-off, he heard one hundred forty voices reply. He certified the count as correct, not having noticed that Heisler was missing. In Heisler's place in the middle of the ranks stood a life-size dummy, attached by its hands to the men on either side of it. The man directly in back of the dummy sang out Heisler's number for it.

Not a flicker, not a sigh of relief came from the disciplined ranks of the prisoners, who knew to a man the trick being employed. Besides, there was still another deception to pass muster and, after that, the most difficult part of all: the walk to the barracks with the dummies.

The second deception worked as smoothly as the first. Leutnant Füllgrabe of Barrack VII stood in for Hochbauer in Barrack V's formation. And in Füllgrabe's place, another of the carpentry shop's artful dummies did duty.

On Howell's order to dismiss, the prisoners broke formation

and headed for their barracks. Unobtrusively, small groups formed around the men walking the dummies, to shield them from the view of the guards. From the waist up, the dummies gave a realistic impression. Below, their legs hung lifelessly. Under the cover of darkness, lost in the mass of eight hundred men, the groups supporting the dummies reached their barracks without incident. Their charges were put to bed, the covers drawn high, only the backs of their heads showing. Wigs borrowed from the prop department of the theatrical group gave these a lifelike appearance.

In Barrack I, Modersohn, with von Sperle at his side, sat at the long pine table, using the hour before "lights out" to compose another coded letter. To be sure that the news he was sending was accurate, he had delayed writing confirmation of the escape until Schmidt and Hochbauer had the full day's leeway he had planned for them. Now their escape could not be detected until the following morning at the earliest. With luck, it might not be detected then. However, Modersohn wasn't one to count on luck. It would be difficult to work the deception in daylight. He had another device to gain more time for the two escapees.

The bugle sounded taps. Von Sperle signed his name to the letter addressed to his mother. It would go into the mailbox first thing in the morning.

In the censhorship room, Gallant stretched as he heard the final bugle call of the day. It had been a tiresome, fruitless day, spent in hurriedly searching letter after letter for hidden meanings that didn't exist.

The euphoria of their easy arrival in Toronto largely dissipated, Schmidt and Hochbauer urgently prowled the city for shelter. Although it was not yet ten o'clock, the aspect of even the midtown area portended the long, dead hours of the night. Already the box offices of the movie theaters were closed and the lights were out on the marquees.

In a side street, an unshaded bulb blinked over a protruding sign: "Rooms." They turned into the street. The sign hung above the narrow door of an unornamented, flat-walled building. Inside, a flight of wooden steps led to a bare landing, poorly illuminated.

"A cathouse," Hochbauer diagnosed.

"How do you know?"

"Extrasensory vibrations. I'm never wrong. They make my balls tinkle."

"Don't get any ideas. It's too dangerous."

As if to emphasize the point, a policeman materialized out of the dark on the opposite side of the street. They tried to appear nonchalant as they strolled on. The policeman crossed the street and looked into the doorway.

The Canadian evening was turning chilly. The pair of escapees covertly eyed the warm, respectable lobby of a luxury hotel. The doorman looked down his nose at them.

"We should have bought suits," Hochbauer grumbled.

Schmidt didn't bother answering. Their instructions had been to buy work clothes proper to the roles they were to play.

The staccato counterpoint of two pairs of high heels overtook them. Hochbauer turned his head.

"Hello, honey," came a throaty voice. "Lonely?"

"No," Schmidt growled.

The wave of perfume that enveloped them as the two girls walked by hit Hochbauer like a blow to the stomach. His muscles contracted and it required a conscious effort not to double over. Whether in pain or ecstasy, he wasn't sure.

"Maybe they have a place," he said in sudden inspiration. "We could spend the night with them."

Schmidt frowned, shaking his head.

"They'd take us to some joint where they rent rooms by the hour."

"They must live someplace themselves. If we offered them enough . . ."

Schmidt reflected. It was the lesser of two evils. And he had no objection to pleasure if it was incidental to duty.

"We'll see," he conceded. "Let me do the talking."

They quickened their pace to overtake the two streetwalkers. They were accosting a solitary man coming from the opposite direction. The man sidled around the girls, who were blocking the sidewalk, shaking his head in embarrassment.

"Change your minds?" asked the girl with the husky voice as Schmidt and Hochbauer approached with obvious intent.

"How much?"

She eyed their clothing.

"Five dollars—apiece."

It was reasonable, but Schmidt hesitated for the form.

"Uh . . . I don't know. You have your own place or do we have to pay for a room, too?"

"The room's cheap, honey." She giggled. "For the time it takes."

"We just got off a ship, baby." Schmidt talked as he imagined a Canadian sailor would. "We want to make a party of it. The whole night."

"For five dollars?" the other girl protested.

"It's twenty dollars for the whole night, mister," her companion rejoined. "And that's a bargain 'cause I got a soft spot for sailors."

"Ten dollars," Schmidt countered.

"Come on, honey, be a sport. Twenty dollars and we'll take you back to our place and give you a real good time."

"No hotel?"

"No hotel, won't cost you a dime extra."

Schmidt was inclined to bargain some more, but he saw the

other girl eyeing the crowd coming out of a movie house for potential customers.

"Okay, twenty bucks. But we stay till morning," he emphasized.

"Honey, you'll get breakfast in bed."

She took his arm. Hochbauer grabbed the other girl. A five-minute walk brought them to a small apartment building, surprisingly shabby-genteel. The two girls shared a one-room studio apartment. After the length of time Schmidt and Hochbauer had spent in communal living, it seemed to provide ample privacy.

"Watch your money," Hochbauer warned Schmidt when the two girls retired to the bathroom together.

"Don't worry," answered the cautious Schmidt. "I'm not going to close my eyes all night."

"Neither am I." Hochbauer grinned lasciviously.

His resolve succumbing involuntarily, Hochbauer was surprised when, a victim of habit, he awakened at 7:30 A.M. to find that he had slept after all. Even while doing so, he had never lost consciousness of the soft, perfumed body curled alongside his own.

Across the room on an identical studio bed, Schmidt lay staring at the ceiling, planning the day. He shook the shoulder of the girl sleeping next to him.

"No," she protested, pulling the blanket over her head, "not in the morning. Go back to sleep."

"Breakfast time," the literal Schmidt answered, uncovering her.

"You want breakfast at this hour"—she grabbed at the blanket—"you get some dumb bitch in a drugstore to give it to you."

Seeing Schmidt about to protest, she pleaded: "You wore me out last night, lover, honest you did."

Mollified, Schmidt got out of bed and settled for a shower and a shave, using a razor he found in the medicine cabinet. Hochbauer followed suit, mindful of the need for an early start. Each one leaving his twenty dollars, they renewed their sensation of liberty as they stepped out of the house onto the city street in search of a drugstore.

It was eight in the morning, the second roll call since their escape was starting.

"I wonder if we've been missed yet?" Schmidt remarked.

A localized heavy spring rain was falling in Bowmanville as the POWs formed for morning roll call. Prisoners and guards alike tended to bury their necks in their collars to hold out the cold trickle of water dripping off their service caps. Anxious one and all to get under cover, the routine was accelerated.

In the gate tower, taking seriously Gallant's suggestion on vigilance, Delamare was voluntarily supervising the proceedings. Sheltered by the overhanging roof of the tower, nevertheless he squinted against the driving sheets of water.

As the evening before, the count-off was concluded without the Canadians' detecting the substitutions. When the order to dismiss was given, the prisoners moved off at a slower pace than usual to accommodate the men supporting the clumsy dummies. For the most part, they walked in groups of six to eight, similar to the groups around the two dummies.

Delamare frowned at the scene below.

"Not in much of a hurry, are they?" he said to the guard standing next to him.

"Yeah, you'd think it wasn't raining."

Picking up the binoculars chained to the railing, Delamare swept the parade grounds, dividing the area into imaginary grids and slowly studying each section. Although he could remark nothing amiss, he kept at it, sensing that there was a reason for the peculiar conduct. Even without the rain the men were normally in more of a hurry and didn't walk in gossiping little groups. They had only fifteen minutes to complete their toilets and attend to personal details before breakfast.

As the men from the three nearby barracks reached their doorways, they were obliged to fall into single file in order to enter. Delamare studied them individually. He could see nothing wrong and switched his attention to the groups heading toward the four barracks in the rear. Swinging his glasses from group to group, he missed the chorus-line entrance to Barrack IV of the two officers and their dummy companion. Unable to pass through the doorway three abreast, they were forced to execute a sideward maneuver.

The occupants of IV and V having reached their quarters, except for some stragglers, Delamare was able to concentrate on those heading for the more distant VI and VII. Barrack VI housed the enlisted men. He paid less attention to it than to VII, where he was shortly presented with a strange spectacle.

A group of six men approached the doorway. The first three men, instead of entering singly, one behind the other, frog-stepped in sideways. The powerful glasses Delamare was using brought the group into close focus. The legs of the center figure did not move. They hung limply, brushing the single step.

With the agility of a wild animal, Delamare turned, letting the binoculars swing free, and bounded down the steep circular staircase. His feet hardly touched the treads. At the bottom he ran almost headlong into Lieutenant Coleman, who was officer of the watch. Coleman was leading a guard detail.

"Sir," Delamare saluted, "request permission to make an immediate search of Barrack VII. May I use your detail? It's urgent."

Coleman nodded his consent without further discussion. A sedentary man, at sea in an active era, he deferred readily to the judgment of the top sergeant.

"On the double," Delamare ordered.

"What is it, Sergeant?" Coleman asked, trotting alongside him.

A lookout in the window of Barrack VII spotted the detail as it crossed the grounds.

"Quick!" he warned. "Delamare's headed this way with a whole squad."

"In the closet," suggested one of the men dismantling the dummy, preparatory to hiding the parts. He picked it up and carried it toward the built-in closets.

"Give it to me!" ordered Kapitänleutnant Kuhn, the barrack leader.

Kuhn took the dummy and carried it into the lavatory, from which he emerged as Delamare, Coleman, and the squad entered.

"Go to it!" Delamare ordered his men, whom he had briefed on the way.

With practiced thoroughness, the men began to search the barrack. Two of them went into the lavatory, where they found several men shaving. One of the cabinets was occupied, as evidenced by a pair of legs showing under the half door. A soldier rapped on the door. There was no response. He opened the door. Seated on the toilet was the dummy.

Barely suppressed laughter from the prisoners greeted the soldier as he entered the dormitory carrying the dummy.

"Okay!" Delamare snapped, addressing Kuhn. "Whose place is this taking?"

Kuhn remained silent.

"Corporal," Delamare ordered the squad leader, "get a list of the prisoners in Barrack VII from the office."

He turned to Kuhn: "We'll have a roll call by name, here on the spot. All you'll accomplish is to miss breakfast."

"Very well, Sergeant." Kuhn pretended to yield reluctantly.

"The dummy was used to take the place of Leutnant Alfred Füllgrabe."

"And where is Füllgrabe?"

Kuhn shrugged, set his lips. Delamare knew it was useless to insist.

"Barrack VII is restricted to quarters," he announced. "You," he ordered one of the soldiers, "stand guard at the door."

"And our breakfast, Sergeant?" Kuhn smiled ironically.

"And our prisoner, Captain?" Delamare mimicked, turned his back, and walked out accompanied by Coleman.

"Good work, Delamare. Now let's get back and put the escape plan into operation," Coleman suggested.

The "escape plan" was the official procedure to be followed in the event of a break. Among other things, the neighboring police forces and the Royal Mounted Police were to be alerted and a description of the wanted man circulated.

"Why don't I stay here with the men in the squad?" Delamare suggested. "We can each take one barrack and see that there's no more funny business going on meantime."

Coleman agreed and marched off briskly. Once beyond the gate, the overweight lieutenant stopped worrying about saving face in front of the prisoners and he broke into a trot. He arrived at Colonel Perry's office, the breath whistling in his throat.

Perry reacted to the news by routing out every available man. Gallant had conditioned him to expect a break but he feared in addition a repetition of the recent riot. The men on duty in the offices were the first troops to be rushed into the compound. Among them were the six men of the censorship staff. Gallant, who had been going through the mail since eight that morning, accompanied them. Shortly thereafter, the rest of the troops, on and off duty, arrived at their emergency stations.

All prisoners outside were herded indoors and details of

guards assigned to conduct a name roll call in each barrack.

In Barracks II and V, Heisler and Füllgrabe stepped forward to answer to the names of Schmidt and Hochbauer. The substitutions went unnoticed by the guards, who did not know the prisoners by name.

In Barrack IV no one answered when the name of Heisler was called. Captain Howell was summoned immediately. He ordered the roll call completed, establishing that Heisler was the only man missing from IV. Next he ordered a search of the barrack. The parts forming the framework and head of the dummy came to light bit by bit, camouflaged among the possessions of the prisoners.

The roll calls in the rest of the barracks were without incident. The troops were withdrawn from the compound and the prisoners allowed to go to the mess hall for a tardy breakfast.

The police posts in the surrounding communities of Bowmanville, Oshawa, and Port Hope were notified by telephone to be on the lookout for Heisler and Füllgrabe. The police chief at Port Hope volunteered the use of two hounds to track the fugitives on the chance they were still in the area.

To circulate the "wanted" order more widely and to handle the distribution of photographs of the fugitives, the federal police were called in.

With the escape plan thus implemented, Colonel Perry summoned Modersohn to his office. Gallant played the role of an observer. It was his first opportunity to see the U-boat ace at close range.

Very poised, Modersohn entered the office, his head held rigidly but noting every detail with a sweep of his eyes.

"Sit down, Captain," Perry said, his tone more of an order than an invitation. In no mood for civility, he didn't do Modersohn the courtesy of introducing him to Gallant.

Not to be treated cavalierly, Modersohn performed a half bow in Perry's direction and another in Gallant's.

"Captain Gallant," said Silent Willi, unable not to flaunt his knowledge of his adversary's identity.

"Captain Modersohn," Perry said severely, "you can spare yourself and your men much gratuitous hardship by cooperating with us."

"We are at war," Modersohn answered sternly. "We are not here to be spared hardships."

"Captain Modersohn," Perry repeated, "I have been extremely lenient in my interpretation of the regulations. If you persist, I shall change my attitude. To begin with, you—and I use the plural you—you will be treated exactly as required by the Geneva Convention. That means your food will be cut to the minimum daily allowance and you will be denied all privileges. Not temporarily, but permanently. There will be no more sports: tennis, swimming, hockey. No more theater, concerts, motion pictures, farming, or walks. The library, the workshops will be closed.

"Those will be the permanent consequences of your actions," Perry threatened. "In addition, I shall mete out punishment to all those directly or indirectly involved in this escape. And the conduct I have witnessed this morning indicates that there is not one man who is not implicated.

"You will all be assembled immediately on the parade grounds and you will remain there until you decide to be 'spared the hardships.' You will remain there without food, may I add."

"You are making things very difficult, Colonel," Modersohn said, continuing to jockey for time for Schmidt and Hochbauer. "You are asking me to betray my men."

"Not at all," Perry countered. "You have no choice but to act in the interest of the majority. No one can call that a betrayal. You can't be blamed for that."

"I am not a child concerned with blame, Colonel," Moder-sohn fenced, knowing Perry's background. "I accept the conse-quences of my acts. But as you say, I have no choice. So . . . I strike my colors for the second time."

With the sparse precision of an action report, Modersohn stated:

"Heisler and Füllgrabe escaped by disguising themselves as Canadian soldiers on a work detail. They climbed the south wall on a ladder yesterday morning between 9:15 and 9:45 in full view of your guards. The precise spot is marked by a freshly cemented crack. That is all I can tell you. I do not know any more for the very good reason that I refused to allow them to discuss their plans with me or with any other person in this camp. You can understand the reason, of course.

"Now, Colonel Perry, I have been candid with you. I trust you will not make my men suffer for that. If there is any pun-ishment to be borne for participation in this escape, I am the one to bear it. The responsibility is mine alone."

"I've no doubt."

Modersohn's eyes flared once, sharply, at the rejoinder. Perry's previous words, spoken in anger and frustration, he had considered largely bluff. But this last sarcasm showed a new awareness on the part of the colonel.

Perry stood up to bring the interview to an end. There was no point in questioning Modersohn further. Modersohn had gone as far as he would.

"So much for our increased vigilance," Perry remarked bit-terly after Modersohn was escorted away from the office by two guards. "They walked out right under the noses of the guards. My fault, really."

"If anyone, or anything, is to blame, it is the rotation system. It does more harm than good."

"That's blaming the tools. One works with what one is given.

I'm afraid I'm not up to the mark. Look at the way I handled Modersohn just now. He knows as well as I do that I don't have the authority to revoke their privileges permanently. I would be called to account by our own people, the Directorate of Prisoners of War. Modersohn was laughing up his sleeve at me. It wasn't until I made the more rational threat of holding them out on the parade grounds that he yielded."

"Did he yield?" Gallant raised an eyebrow. "He gave us a scrap of information which may or may not be the truth. We'll have to check it. At any rate it isn't likely to do us any good. For the rest, he sent us to bloody hell.

"I'm afraid he's stolen the march on us. I thought we could contain him, but you were right. I took too much of a gamble. But the only thing we can do now is carry on with it. If Heisler and Füllgrabe aren't picked up by the police, our only lead to them or—more important—to their project, is through Modersohn."

"Meaning that you don't want me to transfer him."

"Yes."

Perry gestured his resignation.

"You want to look at the outside of the wall or the inside?" Delamare asked Gallant as they left the administration building.

"Outside. No use letting those bastards gloat over us."

"We can drive, then." Delamare indicated a jeep parked nearby. They dashed to it through the rain.

They followed the road as far as the corner of the wall, then turned into the field to circle around it. Delamare drove slowly along the south wall.

"There, I think." Gallant pointed ahead.

They got out to examine the spot.

"Always tell little truths and big lies," he remarked as they viewed the unmistakably fresh ribbon of cement. Ants were scurrying along it. Delamare picked at it with a fingernail. The material crumbled.

"Looks like they couldn't steal enough cement. Must have mixed sugar or flour with it."

"Those the same guards as yesterday?" Gallant indicated the tower fifty yards away where two guards were looking down at them.

"Yeah. Want to speak to them now?"

Gallant nodded. They drove the fifty yards to the tower. Gallant motioned to one of the men who was still observing them.

"Come on down."

The guard walked down the tower staircase to the top of the wall, fifteen feet above them. Without shouting, Gallant was able to verify the rest of the story.

"They took their ladder and everything, Captain." The guard finished his recital on a note of self-defense. "They didn't look as though they were in a hurry or anything. They just walked slow as you please down that road leading to the farm like they had another chore to do down there."

A station wagon turned the corner of the wall and stopped beside them. It was driven by a police sergeant. Two hunting dogs in the back breathed affectionately down his neck. A Veterans' Guard private on the seat next to him called Delamare.

"Sergeant, Captain Howell said you could show us where they took off from."

When the hounds were put on the trail after being given some clothing belonging to Heisler and Füllgrabe to sniff, neither gave any indication of picking up the scent.

"You've tracked up this area too much," the police sergeant complained.

"Can they track in this rain?" Gallant asked.

"Captain, these dogs could track under water." He led his dogs beyond the wall in an effort to pick up the scent there.

"Sure you got the right clothes?" Delamare asked the soldier. "Those foxy bastards could have pulled a switch on you."

"Got them out of their closets, that's all I know."

They watched the police sergeant working his dogs in a semicircle, failing to pick up the scent.

"How about you, Del?" Gallant put in. "You're an old trapper. Couldn't you try to find their trail?"

"Not after a full day has gone by," Delamare smiled. "You've been reading too many stories. There's only one way we're going to find anything; that's by beating the whole area. It'll need a lot of men."

"We'll get them," Gallant answered. "Drive me back to camp."

"I'll keep trying!" the Port Hope policeman shouted as they left.

"It would leave me dangerously understaffed," Perry objected. "And what good could it do? Those men are far from here by now."

"Very likely," Gallant agreed, "but we can't afford to overlook anything.

"We'll never be more than a few miles away from camp," he persuaded. "If there's an emergency, you can have the sirens sounded."

"Well," Perry decided, "I'll let you have fifty men. Take half the administrative staff and draw the rest from the off-duty guards."

The jeep with Gallant, Delamare, the police sergeant, and his two hounds crowded under its dripping canvas hood pulled up on the road leading to the farm. Two trucks loaded with soldiers stopped behind it.

"You organize it, Del," Gallant said.

"I'll just mosey around on my own." The police sergeant asserted his independence.

"Okay, we'll start from here." Del indicated the point where the road disappeared from view of the tower. "That's where the guards last saw them. I'd guess they took to the woods. They'd run into the farm if they went straight ahead or to the right.

"Fall out, you men," Del ordered the soldiers in the trucks. "We're looking for a ladder and a bucket and a couple of trowels. Maybe some uniforms, same as you're wearing. Stay about ten feet apart and keep your lines straight. Sing out if you find anything at all that doesn't look as though it's growing here. And fall in on me if I whistle."

With Delamare and Gallant at either end of the line the search party entered the woods. It was only a few minutes before a shout from a man near Gallant's end of the line halted them.

"Sergeant! Captain! Over here. I found it. The ladder."

"Everyone hold his place!" Delamare ordered as he ran up the line.

They examined the abandoned equipment. Delamare identified the ladder as coming from the backstage of the auditorium. The trowels were handmade of wood covered with tin, artfully crafted to look like real ones and sturdy enough to use. The Port Hope policeman let his dogs scent the material.

"If they got some of this plaster on their shoes," he explained, "the dogs'll be able to track them."

Delamare regrouped the party, spreading them out equally on either side of the discovery. Delamare and Gallant took the center of the line.

"They probably headed for the highway," Delamare conjectured as they started again. "It obliques in over there. They could hit it straight ahead if they were going east or they could circle around the farm to the right if they wanted to head south or west.

"We'll take a straight line from here to the highway and, if we don't find anything, we'll cut back following the highway."

To the accompaniment of occasional curses as someone slipped in the wet underbrush, they proceeded as far as the highway. There, Delamare divided the men in two groups strung out on either side of Highway 2.

The uniforms which Schmidt and Hochbauer had discarded were fallen upon literally by a weary, out-of-condition private of the administrative staff. Stumbling on a protruding root, he skidded face down into the bushes where they lay hidden.

His shouts, first of distress, then of discovery, brought Gallant running from the shoulder of the highway. Delamare arrived a second later from the other side of the highway with the police sergeant and two excited dogs on his heels. Together they examined the uniforms.

Gallant started going through the pockets. Delamare took a pair of trousers, holding them out at arm's length. A puzzled look crossing his face, he put them to his waist, then did likewise with the other pair.

"Look at the size of these. They're made for someone about like me, five feet nine or so."

Gallant looked at him, not comprehending. Delamare explained:

"Didn't you see the descriptions we sent out on Heisler and Füllgrabe? Heisler's just over six feet and Füllgrabe's short and stocky, about five feet five."

Gallant nodded.

"So we're following two different men. Heisler and Füllgrabe, I'll bet you, are sitting back there dry as you please in camp, covering up for a couple of their buddies."

"I knew it couldn't be these dogs. Why, they . . ."

"Supposing you get your dogs following this scent," Gallant interrupted the Port Hope man. "You can go along with him," he said to the two nearest soldiers. "Del, get us back to camp by the shortest route."

CHAPTER 12

While the police of half of Canada and part of the United States were alerted to be on the lookout for men of a description far from theirs, Schmidt and Hochbauer tranquilly went to earth in the easiest fashion possible: they melted into the population. They became indistinguishable from any one of the millions of Canadians pursuing the routine of everyday living.

Their early start on the classified ads secured them a pleasant double bedroom in the home of a lower-middle-class family whose two sons were in the service. By late afternoon, thanks to the war-induced labor shortage, the two Germans were gainfully employed in precisely the jobs they had been instructed to seek.

Schmidt, a former engineering student and a first-class mechanic, was hired in the latter capacity by a small trucking firm. He gave as references some nonexistent garages on the Pacific coast, knowing that no one would bother to check them. After a day's trial, the quality of his work spoke for him.

Hochbauer took on an unskilled job which demanded no references. He became a pump jockey in a small gasoline station whose owner was delighted to have a relief man. His former employee had been drafted a few days before and he had been struggling to maintain a fifteen-hour-a-day operation on his own.

In Bowmanville, without the certainty that Schmidt and Hochbauer were safe, Modersohn endeavored to increase their safety margin, to conceal their identities as long as possible. Schmidt and Hochbauer were essential to his projected mass escape. If they failed, he would have the logistically impossible burden of crossing half of Canada, pursued by every agency in the land, with over two dozen men in tow.

When, in midafternoon, within minutes of Gallant's return, truncheon-bearing Canadian troops marched into the compound, once again Modersohn's instructions had already been issued. The loudspeaker blared orders for all prisoners to return to barracks. Half the men obeyed the order. The other half swapped names, barracks, and in some cases uniforms.

As Modersohn foresaw, the Canadians were not going to hold a simple roll call this time. It was to be an identification parade, a time-consuming procedure rarely resorted to. As each man's name was called, he was required to step forward and his identity was checked against his photograph. Even with the cooperation of the prisoners this was a troublesome undertaking. Most of the photos were bad. They had been taken shortly after capture, and more frequently than not the prisoners had changed considerably in appearance. On capture, they were apt to be exhausted, emaciated scarecrows. A good and plentiful diet plus rest and exercise soon rectified that. To complicate matters further, many prisoners deliberately distorted their faces when being photographed.

In charge of the ID parade, Captain Howell detailed a squad of ten men to handle each barrack. The rest of the troops, comprising every man in Bowmanville, took up stations in the compound, ready to act at the first sight of rebellion. Presupposing a riposte by Modersohn, Gallant accompanied Howell to supervise the parade of Barrack I.

"You will line up in alphabetical order on this side of the barrack"—Howell waved his left hand as he gave the order—"and you will step forward to the table when the corporal calls your name. After, you will go to the other side and remain there until this identification parade is terminated."

In orderly fashion the eighty officers found their places on the side of the barrack indicated by Howell. The corporal laid a file of pictures and identifications on the refectory table. Gallant and Howell stood in back of him. Two men of the squad, one of them an interpreter, were posted in front of the table. The others were at stations around the room.

"Adler, Erich," called the corporal.

A young naval officer stepped to the table. His tanned, rounded face bore little resemblance to the photograph on the table of a sunken-cheeked old-young man. Howell picked it up and held it so that Gallant could see it, too. They studied the hairline, the ears, both of which seemed similar to those of the man standing before them. The eyes, narrow slits, and the nose, apparently with a scab on it, didn't seem the same. They concentrated on the hairline again, looking from the photo to the man until they were sure.

"Next," Howell told the corporal.

"Auersperg, Berthold."

Auersperg stepped forward. If possible, his photograph was worse than Adler's. The face wore a frown, the mouth contorted. Several minutes were required before they could convince themselves that Auersperg was the man in the picture.

The fifth man to be called, Hans Berghaus, dressed in the uniform of an Afrika Korps leutnant, didn't by any stretch of the imagination come close to the person in the photograph. The nose of the latter was definitely short and flat while that of the former was beaked.

"You are not Berghaus," Howell said. "What is your right name?"

The man, who like almost all the prisoners spoke English, turned to the interpreter, asking in German what had been said. The interpreter translated his reply for Howell.

"He says he is Berghaus, sir."

"Tell him he will have ten days of solitary confinement if he refuses to reveal his identity."

"He insists he is, sir," the interpreter replied after an another conference with the prisoner.

Howell had the man taken off to a corner of the room under guard, then raised a quizzical eyebrow at Gallant.

"Fun and games," he said in an undertone. "Methinks this is just the beginning."

Gallant nodded.

"I'm for changing tactics right now."

"Let's try a few more for the form."

Their apprehensions were confirmed within the next few minutes. Runners arrived from all the other barracks with complaints of unidentifiable photographs or outright substitutions. They themselves were at grips with another case.

"Stop this farce," Gallant advised. "We're wasting time."

"I'll have to get orders from the colonel."

"I'll see him," Gallant offered.

Perry sat nervously behind his desk doctoring himself with pills supplied him by Major Farnsworth. His stomach burned and bile constantly rose in his throat. Mindful of the doctor's admonition, he dominated his urge to rant at the news Gallant brought him.

"Very well, halt the parade." Perry's face went white. "We'll resort to more persuasive measures.

"Please have Captain Howell turn them all out on the parade ground immediately. I'll show Modersohn I mean what I say. I'll be down to address them myself.

"Do you approve?" he couldn't avoid adding testily.

Without protest, the prisoners filed out of the barracks into the rain and assembled on the parade ground. Modersohn's command had been explicit: "No violence." There was no reason for risking reprisals which might cause a delay in the construction of the tunnel.

After allowing the prisoners to cool their heels for ten minutes, Perry marched shakily from his office to the compound. The waiting period had been more trying for him than for them.

At the bottom of the staircase to the gate tower where the public-address system was located, Perry halted. Squaring his shoulders, feeling in his uncertainty as though he were mounting to the gallows, he forced his feet to ring out a regular rhythm on the metal steps.

Gripping the microphone, he stared at the assemblage below. He knew that they had followed his slow progress up the staircase, but not one face was turned up to look at him.

"This is Colonel Perry speaking," he announced unnecessarily. "I have one brief statement to make to you." He paused.

"You will remain outdoors on the parade ground until you

decide to cooperate and allow a proper identification parade to be held.

"It is now five o'clock. If you wish to have dinner, you will start cooperating immediately. You will have no food, nor will you be allowed to enter your barracks to sleep or for any other purpose until the identification parade is completed.

"That is all."

He stood for a moment watching for a reaction. No one moved down below. He stared at the tall figure in front of the Barrack I formation. Dramatically, like an Indian fakir, Modersohn lowered himself, back straight, to a cross-legged sitting position on the wet ground. Almost simultaneously every one of his underlings assumed a similar pose.

Perry marched down the staircase with the same measured cadence. His face had the artificial calm of a man who has just received the first warning throb of an incipient cerebral hemorrhage and felt it pass, the precariously balanced calm of a man who cannot afford to be otherwise. Seeing Gallant at the gate, Perry walked toward him.

"I have decided," he announced in a sepulchral tone, "I can no longer procrastinate. I shall remove Captain Modersohn from Bowmanville as soon as this incident is terminated."

Compassionate, reading the strain in his face, Gallant hesitated before replying. Like a sleepwalker, wanting desperately to be alone, Perry didn't wait. He turned and made his way back to his office.

The dinner hour came and passed without any sign of weakening among the prisoners. The rain stopped only to be replaced by the chill of the night. The men uncomplainingly exercised in place to keep warm. They had their orders: "Hold until midnight."

At midnight von Sperle stepped out of ranks and asked to

speak to Captain Howell. The captain came from the gate, where he had set up a command post in a jeep.

"Captain Modersohn will speak to Colonel Perry," von Sperle informed Howell. "He consents to reveal the names of the two men who escaped."

Howell had his orders, too, sent down some hours earlier by Perry after much reflection on how to deal with his opposite number among the prisoners.

"Colonel Perry will not see Captain Modersohn," Howell replied. "If you are ready for the identification parade, we will proceed."

"Agree to the identification," Modersohn told his ADC. The rebuff was no surprise. It would be counter to his own interest to continue resisting for reasons of dubious prestige. The hold-out had already lost him a day's work in the tunnel. That was as much as he could spare. Schmidt and Hochbauer had now had two days' start.

"Use a fine-tooth comb on them," Perry instructed Howell, not without vengefulness. "I don't care if they are out there all night. If necessary, study the photographs under a magnifying glass until you can make an absolute judgment. I don't want any errors this time."

Howell carried out his orders to the letter. Dawn broke over the hungry, shivering group on the parade ground before the examination was completed. The absence of Schmidt and Hochbauer was discovered much earlier, but Howell carried on conscientiously to the last man. The prisoners grumbled but did no more.

Gallant phoned the new descriptions of the missing men to sleepy night-duty officers in the local and federal police posts. At six in the morning he retired to his bed for one sleepless hour. The rain and his fatigue reminded him of his recent illness. He arose with a slight fever, a deep, persistent cough, and a savage detestation of his own weakness—and those of other men as well, Perry's in particular.

In this mood he went to beard the Bowmanville CO in his office before Perry could carry out his intention to transfer Modersohn. The length to which Modersohn had gone to protect Schmidt and Hochbauer made their importance all the more obvious and the surveillance all the more necessary. If that pair were on their way to do sabotage, Modersohn's transfer would not stop them. Of that Gallant was sure.

Instead of resisting, Gallant found Perry surprisingly tractable.

"I might as well tell you," he said as soon as Gallant entered his office, "that I had a call from the Director of Prisoners of War about this escape. We discussed the desirability of transferring Modersohn to another camp." Perry straightened one of his desk pens in its holder. "We decided that, since the situation has deteriorated to its present point, the transfer has lost the efficacy it would have had."

"I stand rebuked," Gallant laughed, partly at Perry's circumlocution.

"Let's hope you stand vindicated." Perry smiled back.

CHAPTER 13

Gallant returned to plugging away at the mail in the censorship room, still his only recourse. That, and police routine, in which he could be of no help, were the paths to be followed. The possibility of tracing the fugitives seemed less promising than ever. The files on both men contained the information that they spoke English perfectly. Obviously they had been well chosen for their task. The only vague clue to them was the fact that they had joined the highway as though they intended to head west or south. The Port Hope police sergeant and his dogs had been unable to track them after the discovery of their uniforms, so this could not be confirmed. Despite the sergeant's boast, the dogs hadn't been able to pick up the scent in the rivers of water running on the shoulders of the highway.

The clerks in the censorship room, who had been on emergency duty in the compound most of the previous day and night, yawned their way through the morning. Gallant joined in their chorus as he continued his search for a possible clue. Sacks of mail now two days old stood waiting for their reluctant perusal.

It wasn't until after lunch that a bleary-eyed private nodding over his reading did a double take and called across the room to Gallant: "Hey, Captain, here's another one of those letters."

On the way to his office to place a call to Kerr, Gallant read the letter from von Sperle to his mother. Its contents were as regimented as the Roman numerals signifying the date. While waiting for the call to be put through to Ottawa, he informed Perry of the intercept.

"What are you up to down there?" Kerr's voice greeted Gallant when the call to Ottawa came through. "I see two of your vultures took wing."

"Yes. That's not what I'm calling about though." Gallant hadn't communicated with Kerr about the escape since he had nothing to add to the routine report which Kerr would see anyway.

"The censorship staff turned up another Irland code letter. If you have someone there who can take dictation in German, I can give it to him over the phone."

"Hold on. I'll put you through to the cipher section. They might as well take it directly."

In less than one hour Kerr was back on the line to Gallant, giving him the decoded message: "Two per plan. Kiebitz ahead schedule."

"Our friend Kiebitz is doing well," Kerr commented. "Last time he was on schedule."

"Yes. Do you read it the same way I do? 'Two per plan' I

take it must mean Schmidt and Hochbauer, that they got away according to plan. Ergo, that plan isn't Kiebitz. Maybe it has nothing to do with Kiebitz since Kiebitz is ahead of schedule and they're just on, if you can take 'per plan' to mean 'on schedule.'"

"Could be," Kerr answered. "It's the 'ahead of schedule' that worries me. They're gaining momentum."

"I know. I can feel it in the air . . . the way they were prepared for the ID parade.

"Any objection to sending this letter on?"

"No, no objection. But, uh, we might run into some static about the whole operation. I had a call this morning from the Director of Prisoners of War. Usual upper-echelon politics . . . getting ready to say 'I told you so.'"

"He already did." Gallant related the conversation he had had with Perry that morning.

"I think Perry and I have reached a *modus vivendi,* though," Gallant ended.

The *modus vivendi* was sufficiently durable to have Perry accept, even with gratitude, suggestions Gallant came up with, after a night's sleep, to plug the loopholes in Bowmanville's defenses.

Amazed and dismayed at the utter chaos of the identification parade, Gallant diplomatically told the colonel he had some measures in mind to avoid such "confusion" in the future.

"In case we need to identify the men again, we should have a method of sorting them out rapidly," he suggested. "To start with, we should have decent photographs made."

"Yes," Perry assented. "I think, after my conversation with the director, I could get a budget allocation for that."

"Immediately?"

"Well, it might require a bit of time." Perry admitted with a slight smile. "I'll have the photographs made and then do a bit of administrative juggling."

"Fine," Gallant encouraged. "Of course, the photographs by themselves won't do the job. The guards should know the prisoners by name. We could assign eighty guards the duty of memorizing the identity of ten prisoners apiece, all from the same barrack. If we have another case of barrack switching, the guards could sort out the men they know and send all the interlopers outside. Then we could march them past the guards in single file and weed them out. It should be a relatively rapid operation."

"Hmm," Perry considered, "quite practical. Why not?"

"It's practical up to a point," Gallant led him on. "The Director of Prisoners of War will have to agree to stop rotating the troops every three months to make it really effective."

"Good heavens," Perry said, using his closest approach to profanity, "you don't expect this situation to last that long? We won't rotate the guard for almost another three months."

"I hope things are cleared up before then. But in case they aren't, I'm sure you wouldn't want to put in the request at the last moment. Better to give the director plenty of time to rearrange his schedule."

"I suppose it is better to err on the side of caution. Believe me, I thoroughly approve of everything you've suggested. Are there any other measures?"

"One. Could you place a guard, two if you can spare them, at the door of each barrack after roll call? That would put an end to the use of dummies and perhaps to some other tricks we haven't thought of."

"Agreed."

As the measures were put into effect, the prisoners' intelligence service caught wind of them. The only precaution of any annoyance to Modersohn was the posting of guards at the barrack doors. It meant changing the shifts of the crews in the tunnel. Men from other barracks could no longer enter Barrack III immediately after roll call. More serious than this inconvenience was the indication that the Canadians were becoming more vigilant.

Yet, Silent Willi laughed to himself, considering his recent activity the new measures were hardly surprising. The Canadians must have the wind up properly, as the British in Grizedale Hall used to say. Not that it would do them any good. He wasn't concerned with concealing the break once it was made. A mass break was impossible to conceal for long. At the latest, his would be discovered at morning roll call. But he wasn't counting on that. One hour would see him through.

Despite the reports he continued to receive every day that week on the new Canadian measures, Modersohn remained optimistic. The work on the tunnel was progressing splendidly. He calculated that, at the present rate, it would be completed five days before it was needed.

His fourth day on the job as a gasoline-station attendant, Hochbauer left the house at the same hour as Schmidt although he was on a noon-to-9-P.M. shift. The chore he was to accomplish that morning gave him more pleasure than anything he had done since before the war. He was on his way to buy a motorcycle.

Among the skills for which Hochbauer had been selected by Modersohn was his ability at the handlebars. In his teen-age civilian days Hochbauer had led the field in cross-country racing and hill climbing.

Traveling downtown with Schmidt, Hochbauer veiled his exuberance. Schmidt was a strict service type, probably inherited it from his old man, the consul. Not one you could talk cycles to. He wouldn't understand the feeling it gave a man to be astride a cycle again, even one of the heavy American machines like the police in Canada used. It was on a par with being astride that whore the first night out of camp, Hochbauer thought, a grin flickering on his face. But Schmidt had done that only in the line of duty. Glad to be on this particular mission alone, Hochbauer jumped off the bus near the Harley Davidson showroom, leaving Schmidt to continue on to work.

No new machines were available, the salesman told him regretfully. Used ones were scarce, too, but they did have a few. Resisting temptation, Hochbauer turned down the salesman's offer of a trial run. He limited himself to spinning the machines around the courtyard of the garage. He was not to risk an accident or a traffic violation.

Finally, Hochbauer selected the one machine that had almost new tires. It was also the least expensive, being in poor mechanical shape. That could be put right with one day's labor. The salesman assured him the agency had a complete line of spare parts in stock.

The agency volunteered to procure the license for the cycle, sparing Hochbauer unnecessary dealing with officialdom. He paid in cash—two hundred seventy-five dollars—and arranged to take delivery the following day.

Hochbauer's boss consented to his storing the machine in the rear of the station. He was not to drive it for personal use, but with gas rationing no one considered it strange that he used it infrequently. His first day off, Hochbauer used the station's tools and facilities to overhaul the Harley Davidson thoroughly.

Two weeks after quitting Bowmanville, Hochbauer was back again—on the outside. Leaving Toronto at six in the morning on his reconditioned motorcycle, he loafed along in the sunshine of the early July morning, taking over an hour to make the thirty-odd–mile run. He arrived in the vicinity of Bowman-ville shortly after 7 A.M., long before anyone from the camp was at work on the farm or walking through the woods.

Confident as an adolescent in his ability to outdistance any-thing on wheels, particularly in rough country, Hochbauer turned into the side road leading to the former reformatory with the insouciance of an old boy on a visit. At the fallen tree he had reconnoitered with Schmidt and Krafft, he halted his machine. Leaning forward in the saddle, his head cocked to one side as it might be if he were listening to the throb of his idling engine, Hochbauer surveyed the surrounding woods. Seeing no one, he dismounted, kicking down the brace for the cycle to lean on. He drew a cigarette package from his pocket. A Chesterfield package. Extracting the last cigarette, he crum-pled the pack, putting the cigarette between his lips. Then, placing a foot on the fallen tree, he bent over as though tying his shoelace. His hand reached into the hollow spot he had pointed out to his companions. It was empty—no emergency message that would change their schedule. He opened his hand, leaving the crumpled cigarette package in the hollow.

His mission accomplished, Hochbauer straightened up, casu-ally stretched, lighted his cigarette and stepped back to his ma-chine. One kick and the motor came to life. Hochbauer jounced back to the highway, unseen.

At a later hour that morning, Krafft and a companion in-dulged in an innocent habit they had formed a few days ear-lier. During their walk on parole, they would take a cigarette break for a few minutes, sitting on the fallen tree by the road-side, lounging away the time that weighs so heavily on prison-ers. Restless, Krafft would toy with the earth behind the log, letting it run through his fingers as a farmer might.

This time his nervous exploring fingers touched the crumpled

Chesterfield package. He played with it, tossing it in the air and catching it as he and his companion got up and strolled into the woods. Smoothing it out, Krafft verified that the inside wrapping had been torn precisely in half, then he tossed the package away. There was nothing in it. Only in an emergency would there have been a written message. Otherwise, the non-incriminating bit of refuse sufficed. Its presence said that Schmidt and Hochbauer had not been recaptured and were in a position to carry out their assignment.

Modersohn received the message imperturbably. He bobbed his head once at Krafft and it seemed as though the news was of no importance to him. Actually, it was a day he had been awaiting under maximum pressure, but Silent Willi had no safety valve to blow steam. Not even a smile.

It was also a day that Gallant had been awaiting, with diminishing optimism. The incoming mail that day contained a letter to von Sperle, purportedly from his mother. The date was in the by now familiar Roman numerals.

Waiting for Kerr to call back with the decoded message Gallant sat impatiently at his desk in his cubbyhole, which was too small for any serious pacing. When the call came, he heard in Kerr's voice a note of excitement that had never entered it before.

"Gallant?" Kerr's voice boomed to offset a poor connection.

"Yes."

"You got yourself the right-hand lead this time."

"The what?"

"Right-hand lead. Big story."

"What is it?" Gallant had to ask the exuberant Kerr, who usually rapped out his messages like a telegraph key.

"Twenty-eight of your playmates are homesick so their old man is sending a couple of their favorite toys to pick them up,"

Kerr said, adding immediately: "Come on in. It's something we'll have to discuss."

"Okay. But did what you just said mean what I think it does?"

"There's only one interpretation," Kerr assured him.

"And one response?"

"And one response," Kerr repeated. "That's why I want you to come in. I'm setting up a conference. As a matter of fact, bring your colonel. It'll make it easier later on."

"It certainly will. Is there anything to be done on this end before we leave? When's the regatta?"

"Didn't say, but I don't think they're treading on our tails. They'd have to leave a little leeway. The postal service doesn't promise rapid delivery on their category of mail."

"Good, then we can leave here without sounding the tocsins."

"Definitely. And if you think explanations will make trouble, don't give any. Just say 'orders' and bundle the old boy in a car. If you leave now, you should make it in by ten. But don't kill yourselves. I'll be briefing the others first anyway."

CHAPTER 14

Like many elaborate precautions, the excuse which Gallant prepared for Perry was unnecessary. Perry himself supplied an out when Gallant indicated that the urgent summons from Kerr concerned a top-secret matter.

"Tell me about it in the car," the colonel cautioned, motioning toward the beaverboard wall separating them from the outer office.

Efficiently, Perry gave his last-minute orders to Captain Howell and was ready to leave in twenty minutes. Gallant stuffed some clean linens and his toilet gear into a briefcase and met the colonel in front of the administration building, where his staff car was waiting.

As Gallant sped the olive-drab sedan out of camp, he was observed by the prisoner on watch duty opposite the gate. As a result, Modersohn spent a bad night pondering the reason for the precipitous departure of the intelligence officer and the camp commander on the heels of Hochbauer's trip that morning. Hochbauer could have been picked up or met with an accident. True, he wasn't likely to talk. The Canadians were not at all enterprising in encouraging confessions.

The speed at which Gallant drove over the side road was well above that which the colonel permitted his driver. The bouncing car made conversation difficult and it wasn't until they turned onto the highway that Perry cleared his throat indicatively.

"Ah." He craned to read the speedometer. "If you are adept enough to converse at this speed, we might . . ."

"Yes, of course. The speed doesn't disturb you, does it? Kerr is expecting us around ten."

"No, no, I don't mind. Rather exhilarating as a matter of fact. One doesn't usually have a valid reason for it."

Gallant glanced at Perry. He was not being facetious. The severe lines on his face had softened and he was obviously savoring this, for him, unusual adventure.

"From what Kerr told me, we have a legitimate reason, all right. I think, Colonel, we're going to have an opportunity to turn the tables on our friends in Bowmanville. We've finally discovered what they're planning and it seems quite likely we'll be able to turn it to our advantage."

This time it was Perry who took his eyes off the road, which he had been staring at as concentratedly as if he were at the wheel. He looked at Gallant and smiled slightly.

"It's all right, Captain. I'm not a cardiac case. You may come to the point."

"All right." Gallant chuckled. "I'll give it to you in one take.

Twenty-eight men from Bowmanville have a rendezvous with two U-boats which are being sent over to pick them up. We don't know when or how they are planning to get out of Bowmanville. Or where they are going to meet the U-boats. But somehow or other we intend to discover all that and be there with a welcoming committee."

As he spoke, Gallant's eyes flicked from the road to Perry. The colonel listened with the concentration of a concertgoer—absorbing everything, but with composure.

"I couldn't discuss things openly with Kerr on the phone," Gallant continued, "so part of what I've told you I merely deduced."

"Have you also deduced how the discovery of the rendezvous will be made?" Perry asked shrewdly.

"I can give you my own idea on it. If we're lucky, we'll intercept some more coded letters mentioning that. If not, the only means I can think of is to use the prisoners as bait."

"To deliberately let them escape?" Perry's tone was more reflective than incredulous. "Do you really believe it is feasible?"

"That's what we'll have to decide tonight."

They both fell silent, watching the underpopulated never-ending expanse of Canada, thinking of the problems involved in following twenty-eight men unobserved through such country.

"Twenty-eight men," Perry reflected after a while. "That's a large group. It could become quite nasty. Dangerous, twenty-eight men organized to break out of camp. No telling what they'll try."

"It might be dangerous. But if we stop them, we lose an excellent chance to sink two U-boats."

"Good heavens, Captain, I wasn't thinking of stopping them. It may surprise you, but I regard the sinking of two U-boats as more important than the maintenance of the status quo in my camp. By the way, why are two U-boats being sent for twenty-eight men?"

"Well, they're hardly passenger liners. Have you ever seen the inside of one?"

"No, I haven't."

"There's literally hardly enough space to turn around. There isn't even enough room for the crew to have individual bunks. They share them: one shift sleeps while the other works. I'm fairly certain they'll have to strip the boats to accommodate the extra men . . . meaning they won't be able to make it an operational cruise at the same time. Those twenty-eight men must be highly valued."

Perry said, "Mmhmm," and fell silent, contemplating the problems he would have to face. Gallant stepped up the speed of the sedan another ten miles an hour, his mind whirling at the same pace as he organized his thoughts.

By the time Gallant and Perry arrived in Ottawa—about a half hour ahead of schedule—Kerr had the bureaucratic snarls out of the project which required interservice cooperation as well as the tacit approval of the United States and England.

A cloud of tobacco smoke erupted from Kerr's office as Miss Griffon opened the door for Perry and Gallant. One of his black cigarettes bobbing between his lips, Kerr introduced them to the navy and the federal police representatives assigned to the project: Commander John MacLevy of the Royal Canadian Navy, who had the competent nonservice look of a blue-water racing skipper, and Captain Peter Caspery of the Royal Canadian Mounted Police, whose countenance was stamped with a permanent air of suspicion.

Considerably bothered by the smoke, Perry attempted to shake hands while at the same time massaging an irritated eye. For his benefit, Gallant read aloud from the sheet of paper which Kerr tossed to him across the desk.

" 'Tanker unavailable. Sending U-536, U-841. Assign twelve men 536, sixteen 841. Location, date agreeable.' "

"That's it. The whole story," Gallant addressed Perry, who was wiping his other eye as he nodded his understanding.

"Commander MacLevy here tells me," Kerr explained, "that a U-boat tanker—which is a supply boat as well—would have enough space to accommodate twenty-eight men. According to our intelligence reports, the Germans do not have a shortage of tankers, so unless they are wrong, there must be another reason for the tanker not being available. Perhaps a buildup some-place. Anyway, it's a break for us. We get a crack at two boats.

"The U-536, again according to Commander MacLevy, is what's known as a VII-C boat. You don't mind, by the way, MacLevy, my taking the floor?"

"Not at all." MacLevy waved him on.

"A VII-C boat," Kerr recited the technical details with pleas-ure, "is a five-hundred-tonner and carries a crew of forty-seven. The U-841 is a Type IX, a seven-hundred-ton class with a crew of sixty-eight.

"That explains the uneven assignment of passengers. They both would be filled to the scuppers by the extra men.

"Unfortunately, the last part of the message isn't as informa-tive as the first. Colonel Perry, this places you on the firing line. We're going to have to allow your prisoners to escape in order to trace them to the boats."

"I had an intimation of that already, sir," said Perry stoically. "You've . . . uh . . . cleared it with the Directorate of Pris-oners of War?"

"Spoke to the director this afternoon," Kerr reassured him.

"Supervising the escape is going to be the most delicate part of the operation. The slightest suspicion on their part could not only lose us the subs but the prisoners as well. Captain Caspery was just telling us some of the difficulties we could run into in trailing them. It's absolutely essential that we be onto them from the very start. Properly organized, we can stick with them. But if we ever let them get away . . ." Kerr raised his hands. "You all are familiar with our topography. They could lose themselves in the wilds and we'd have a hell of a time picking them up again. The local police aren't very well equipped to help us, either. Lack of communications for one thing. There's no such thing as a police teletype hookup like in the cities. It will mean separate phone calls to hundreds of little communities to keep them abreast of the hunt."

Kerr turned toward Perry and Gallant, got as far as saying, "You two," and stopped to beat the live ash of his cigarette butt off his shirt. He unpasted the stub from his lip, got another cigarette going, and continued.

"The operation starts at your end. Supposing you tell us how you think it might be handled. Gallant, you'll also be coordinating the whole business."

"That's your department, Captain." Perry waved. "I'll give you all the cooperation I can, but the strategy end is very much out of my sphere. There is one question I'd like to raise, though. Since we know the code, wouldn't it be possible to send a letter purporting to come from von Sperle suggesting a new rendezvous? There are pretexts which could be found for that."

"Yes, that's not the difficulty," Kerr answered him. "We were very tempted to do so, but we had to reject the idea because of one stumbling block. Before the U-boats come in for a landing —probably before they even surface—the prisoners very likely will flash them a recognition signal. MacLevy tells us that would be fairly standard procedure. Since we don't know the signal and we're not one-hundred-percent sure there is one, we're bound to put our foot in it. We can't ask for a new signal if we don't know that there is an old one. The only pretext we could have for a new signal anyway is that there has been a leak, and that might put them off the whole operation."

"Sorry," Perry put in humbly. "As I told you, this isn't my sphere."

Kerr waved off his apology. "It's been said already, Colonel, this is a layman's war.

"Gallant?"

"To begin with," Gallant responded, "can I assume we'll get everything we need or are we second string? If we are, I think we'd better reexamine our position."

"Let's hear what you need," Kerr answered. "Within reason I can badger anything."

"Our first requirement is a perimeter guard on the outside of the camp. Their job will be to spot the prisoners when they break out. We can't use the guards we have now. There aren't enough of them and they aren't the right type." He turned to address Perry. "While we're on the subject, will you require more guards?"

"We certainly could use them, but I think it would be wiser to forego them. They would give our hand away. The prisoners would notice the increase immediately."

Gallant reflected. "Combat intelligence squads are the sort we'll need for the perimeter guard," he went on. "Four competent squads should do the trick. Men who have been trained in field operations and camouflage. They'll have to let the escape party pass right over them if necessary.

"We'll want them in civilian clothing. There'll be times when they won't be under cover and the prisoners have spotters outside the camp as well as inside. Unfortunately we can't at this point discontinue their outside activities—the farm, the walks on parole. The day shift is going to be particularly difficult.

"Normally, most breaks are made at night. Particularly mass breaks. But there have been successful escapes made during the day. Last week's, for instance. It involved only two men, but nothing would be simpler than for a large group to make a daylight break while out on parole. I know that's supposedly never done—violating the code—but I think some of them would violate their mothers if it served their purpose.

"Usually, though, mass breaks are made through tunnels and at night. If there is a tunnel being dug, we might stumble on some sign of it. Colonel, your guards will have to be warned to play dumb if they accidentally find something. That means they'll have to be told about this operation. Do you think we can rely on them? I'm not impugning their loyalty, but some of them do talk rather freely with the prisoners."

"There are a few whose tongues and brains do lack coordination," Perry agreed. "We'll do a thorough weeding job. My staff is well aware of them."

"Good then," Gallant resumed. "Now, once the prisoners are out and beyond the perimeter guard, we'll need a crew of specialists to tail them. Counterintelligence men perhaps, or police detectives. We'll need four two-way radio cars stationed around the camp, night and day. They'll establish the first contact and relay it on to other teams. I presume you'll step in there, Captain Caspery."

Caspery, who had been making approving nods during Gallant's exposition, gave his confirmation.

"I've got a damn strong hunch," Gallant said, grimmacing, "these men are going to travel by road. It's the most practical way. And they are practical, and well organized. We can take it for granted they've made their travel plans. They wouldn't leave that up to chance. They're going to have to move fast and cover a long distance.

"Trains and buses wouldn't meet their needs very well. Too large a group. They'd have to split up in order not to be spotted. They'd also have difficulty getting to the train or bus, and it wouldn't take them directly to their destination, which has to be a deserted stretch of shore. One man might get through that way, not twenty-eight.

"They could hijack a plane." Gallant's tone indicated he didn't think much of this method either. "It would be possible to find a beach to land it on. But, well, I don't have to go into the difficulties of hijacking a plane.

"They also could get hold of a boat some way or other, but where could they go with it? Across the lake to the States and they'd still have a land-transportation problem after. If they tried going up the St. Lawrence to the sea, there'd be too many points where they could be bottled up, . . . canals, bridges."

"They can be bottled up on the road, too," MacLevy objected.

"There's always another road," Gallant answered. "And the highway is a common means of transportation. They can hope to pass unobserved.

"But the point I've been leading up to is that they'll very likely have outside help. In addition, that is, to what they have from Germany. With minor variations, most things run pretty true to form. The most successful jail breaks I've covered have been done with the aid of a car waiting right outside the prison walls. That's what I suspect is being planned here.

"I don't know if you two are aware of it"—he indicated MacLevy and Caspery—"but the two prisoners who got away from Bowmanville last week haven't been recaptured. We know they were given some sort of mission to accomplish, and there's a possibility they might have had over a thousand dollars to do it with.

"Since all we have to go on are presumptions and guesses, we'd better keep an eye on the possibility that Schmidt and Hochbauer may be waiting outside Bowmanville with one or two large vehicles, trucks or buses, enough to transport twenty-eight men.

"Oh, by the way," Gallant added. "Can we cancel the pickup

order on Schmidt and Hochbauer and just maintain a lookout for them?"

"Right, I'll take care of it," Kerr said.

"That's all then," Gallant answered.

"Caspery?" Kerr called on the federal police captain. The MP took a last long puff on his cigarette, stubbed it out in an ashtray, and exhaled forcefully.

"We can have several radio cars in the area to relay those you'll have set up on the highway," he began. "After we know the direction they're taking, we'll telephone ahead to our posts and to the local police to be on the lookout for them. Also to the American police if they head down that way. If we try to tail them too closely in rural areas, they'll be on to us. All we can do is check them through certain points. We should be able to box them in fairly well. Where we'll have to play it very close is when they get down on the shore itself. The danger is that they'll hole up between two checkpoints. Supposing we back them up with a car that remains a mile or two behind them? When they stop, our car will pass within a couple of minutes—before they can get under cover. How does that sound?"

"Okay to me," Kerr said.

"That covers my end of the business then," Caspery said crisply.

"MacLevy?" Kerr eyed the commander.

MacLevy got up from his chair and walked over to a map of Canada hanging on the wall.

"We've got a long coastline"—he pointed—"and a busy navy. We can't have ships lying idle for weeks or months in every spot where they might come in. Even if we had nothing else to do, there still wouldn't be enough ships.

"Of course, once your prisoners get under way we should have a general idea of the area they're headed for. We have coastal-patrol vessels that we'll try to get into position for an intercept, but there may not be time. We may have to depend on aviation. Ships would be preferable, particularly at night— and I should think they'll try for a night landing. However, we are doing a fairly creditable job on low-level night bombing now," the commander reassured them.

"As to the ships, we'd want to get them in while the U-boats are surfaced close to shore, particularly in the Gulf of St. Lawrence. I don't know if you are aware of it, but we've never managed to sink a U-boat anywhere in the St. Lawrence. The gold braid keeps it rather hush-hush, though it's certainly no secret to the Germans. Question of pride, I suppose. We can't count on tracking your boats if they have time to submerge. The underwater currents in the area muddle our asdic. The currents have different temperature levels than the water around them and they bounce the asdic beams back more or less like a sub does."

"Wouldn't it be possible," Kerr suggested, "to concentrate some naval forces in the areas most favorable for a landing? For instance, if you were commanding one of the U-boats, what spot would you choose?"

MacLevy searched the ceiling as he considered the question. Taking a ruler from Kerr's desk, he placed it on the map, one end at Bowmanville, and traced a direct line to the sea. The ruler crossed Lake Ontario, bisected the state of New York, continued through the bottom of Vermont and New Hampshire and the top of Massachusetts to hit the Atlantic Ocean near the port of Gloucester.

"There's the shortest line. It means crossing the border into the United States, though."

"Not impossible," Gallant interjected.

"There you are," MacLevy concurred. "That's what I wanted to point out. There are thousands of spots and you can make out a good case for almost any one of them.

"We've alerted the Americans and, if they head down that

way, they'll take over—which brings us back to our own terri-
tory.

"If I were a U-boat skipper, the Gulf of St. Lawrence would
appeal to me most for the reasons I just mentioned. Quebec
province would make as good a spot as any for the boats. For
the prisoners it would be a longer haul than cutting straight
through to New Brunswick, but it would give them the advantage of not having to run the gauntlet crossing the St. Lawrence River. They could be captured quite easily at one of the
bridges or ferries.

"The river, by the way," MacLevy said, arching an eyebrow,
"is a possibility we don't want to overlook. U-boats have penetrated it and, in at least one case, used it to land saboteurs. I'm
speaking of the upper reaches, of course.

"If the prisoners choose to cross the river, they have all this
area for their rendezvous." He pointed to the coastline of New
Brunswick. "There's Chaleur Bay and this strip down to Miramichi Bay, hundreds of good landing spots there. After that,
Northumberland Strait. Prince Edward Island lies off the coast
there, which means they couldn't make a direct run for the
open ocean, but there is plenty of navigating room in the strait.

"The one spot I wouldn't choose is here," he said, pointing to
the Bay of Fundy. "Highest tides in the world. And Nova
Scotia is on the other side, so they'd have to make a run around.
Of course, they might select it precisely because one wouldn't
expect it.

"Does that answer your question, sir?" MacLevy smiled apologetically at Kerr.

"Yeah," Kerr growled. "We haven't a clue."

He studied the four men grouped around his desk, calculating the risk involved.

"We're going to have to get on their tail and stay on it. The
twenty-eight men in this affair are important enough to the

enemy to risk two U-boats for them. This escape wasn't arranged for a lark or to spring someone's favorite. Not with that many men involved.

"If at any time you have to choose between losing their trail or perhaps blowing the whole deal, blow it. We're not gambling. We're rigging the odds in our favor. We can afford to let them take a little organized tour in order to sink two subs. But we can't afford to let them escape.

"These are categorical orders. Those men are not to board the U-boats under any circumstances. And I mean machine-gun them if necessary. You can count on the subs firing back so don't waste time worrying about shooting unarmed men.

"Gallant, you'll have your men and equipment tomorrow . . . Today," he corrected, looking at his watch.

At five in the morning, not having given sleep a thought, Gallant and Perry arrived back at Bowmanville, the valves of the staff car floating after being driven over four hours, accelerator pressed to the floorboard. No prisoner was on hand to report their return to Modersohn. At the guardhouse a suddenly alert corporal reported that nothing out of the ordinary had happened during the night.

During the next twenty-four hours they put into action the plans they had discussed in Kerr's office.

The weak links among the guard were shifted to maintenance duties; the others were thoroughly briefed and cautioned by Perry in his most impressive manner.

When the combat intelligence squads and four radio cars arrived late that afternoon, Gallant, largely on Delamare's suggestions, already had their posts scouted out. Working all that night, they were entrenched in camouflaged positions by the following morning. Equipped with walkie-talkies, the squads were in communication with Gallant's command post and with the four radio cars assuring the second line of defense on the roads surrounding the camp.

Caspery phoned in to report that a network of police from Bowmanville to the coast was already on a stand-by alert. Kerr and MacLevy also confirmed the setup of their parts of the counterplot.

Operating on his own initiative, Delamare brought in proof that the escape was being planned via a tunnel. Experienced in the devices employed by POWs, Delamare found his evidence in the garbage dump.

"What's this, garbage inspection now?" one of the privates on the trash truck complained when Delamare intercepted them as they entered the dump.

"Just want to take a look at your load," Delamare explained, getting out of his jeep.

"You what? Christ, Sergeant, we ain't trying to make off with the old man's silver. You ribbing us?"

"Which cans are from the prisoners' mess? Do you know?"

"Yeah. We pick them up first. They're in the back. The ones in front are from our mess. Think we got an escaped prisoner hiding in one of them?"

"Start dumping," Delamare ordered. "And take it easy when you come to the prisoners' cans. I want to see what's in them."

The two privates shrugged and did as ordered.

"There are no tin cans in any of this," Delamare pointed out when they had dumped the prisoners' garbage. "Did you ever notice that before?"

"Hell, Sergeant, we dump this crap; we don't put our noses in it."

"Those guys in the camp are probably using them for chamber pots. They got it so soft here they're probably too lazy to get up at night to take a leak."

Delamare had a more rational explanation.

"I should have thought of it a long time ago," he told Gallant. "We've all seen how they use tin cans when they're digging tunnels. They string them together to make a ventilating system.

"I've been looking to see where they're dumping the earth, too, but I can't spot it. Must be indoors someplace. If you could get them out of the barracks for some reason or other, I could make an inspection without disturbing anything. We could find out exactly where the tunnel is located."

"If they suspect anything, it'll make it harder to follow them. We'll sit tight," Gallant decided.

CHAPTER 15

Edward and Clement Alger, owners of Alger Bros. Transport Lines, touched wood every time they spoke of their new employee, Walter Crowninshield. He would have been a find at any time, but to have him drop into their laps during the wartime manpower shortage was a miracle. He was an extraordinarily skilled mechanic, prompt, willing to work overtime, half the night if necessary. Unlike others of his trade, he didn't waste time running out for coffee or a drink every hour or chewing the rag with the other men. Despite this, his shopmates liked him. He was always ready to lend a hand.

The Algers understood that such a man would be ambitious. They even found it commendable, although they hoped it wouldn't lead him to set up his own shop. When Crowninshield bought a secondhand truck, saying he wanted to resell it to make some extra money, they gladly gave him permission to garage it on their premises and to work on it there on his own time. Anything, as long as he didn't leave.

After the other men left at night, Crowninshield stayed alone in the garage working on his truck. It had to be perfect. Every piece of the motor, the transmission, the rear end, the steering had to come out to be checked for wear or defects. There could be no breakdown on the voyage this truck was to make. Crowninshield also made modifications General Motors hadn't thought necessary. An extra fuel tank gave the vehicle an autonomous cruising range of fifteen hundred miles. A strengthened front bumper made it capable of ramming its way through a roadblock and two steel plates on the lower part of the rear doors provided a minimum immunity from bullets.

As a prudent man should, Crowninshield kept his truck locked. No prying eyes ever saw the modifications or the signs he later made and stored in the closed van. Nor did the Alger brothers or their drivers notice the trifling amounts of gasoline he siphoned from the company trucks every night. It wasn't enough to fill his tanks but every drop helped circumvent the rationing problem.

Christian Foucauld, in his gasoline station, had more varied means of fueling Crowninshield's vehicle. Safest was the oldest trick known to pump jockeys: a fast withdrawal of the hose before the last glassful of fuel flowed into the customer's tank. There was also the occasional careless customer who handed him an extra ration coupon by error and the imprudent ones who didn't check the amount being delivered.

On the pretext of keeping his motorcycle in condition, Foucauld would take it out for a spin every few nights. He would run it as far as the garage where his roommate, Crowninshield, was working on his truck. Strapped to the side of the cycle were two five-gallon jerrycans. Little by little, the truck's tanks gurgled toward repletion.

By the end of August, Schmidt and Hochbauer were ready to pull up stakes, materially and spiritually. Their tasks in Toronto were completed. The truck and the motorcycle were in better than new condition. Locked in the former were food, drink, and changes of clothing for all the men. The clothing was for another of Modersohn's alternatives. If the escapees were forced to abandon the truck, they were to continue their flight individually by whatever means presented itself.

Life in Toronto as escaped POWs was not so amusing as Schmidt and, more particularly, Hochbauer might have wished. Their necessarily circumspect conduct gave them little more liberty than they had had in Bowmanville. In a way, it was worse. Everything was so tantalizingly at hand; they could see other people partaking of the pleasures they themselves yearned for, yet could not touch. With their preparations accomplished, each day of waiting loomed fretfully large.

In Bowmanville as August ended, the conspirators on both sides of the wall lived each day with mounting tensions. The Canadians waited impatiently, bored by the routine yet unable to relax, not knowing when the attempt would be made. Certainly before the cold of autumn.

Inside the compound, enthusiasm mingled with impatience. A strata of soft earth and a home-stretch sprint completed excavation of the tunnel on September 2, nine days ahead of schedule. All that remained to be done was to break through the few feet separating the shaft from the surface.

On September 8, the beautiful sunny weather which had held all summer changed. An early hurricane swept in from the south, gathering force over Lake Ontario and hitting the shore communities with driving winds and rain.

Modersohn posted a man to listen to all the weather-bureau

reports on the clandestine radio hidden in the tunnel entrance. The reports were unchangeable. The wind was expected to abate within twenty-four hours but the rain was not expected to let up for two or three days.

Relaying the weather news to his chief, von Sperle knew better than to pose questions, but Modersohn, aware of the tension among his men, broke his habitual silence.

"We go anyway. You may tell the men. The rain is in our favor. The police will be busy and less vigilant."

He didn't mention to von Sperle his concern that floods or washouts might block their route. Unless a last-minute report indicated that the roads were impassable, they would leave. He had no way of calling off Schmidt and Hochbauer. If their comrades failed to appear, Schmidt and Hochbauer were to return for four successive nights, but it would greatly increase their collective peril.

The winds howling in over Bowmanville the first day of the storm sought every crevice in the buildings and made the stone barracks chill and damp. In a few of the barracks it lifted up the roof shingles, letting water trickle into the attics. Not much rain got through, however. Not enough, at any rate, to drip through the ceilings and be noticed.

Perhaps the shingles of Barrack III were damaged more than the others. A week earlier on a particularly hot afternoon, two officers, without orders, had shifted a number of shingles to one side to let in some fresh air. They replaced them hurriedly at the end of their shift.

Or perhaps this had nothing to do with it; perhaps a trickle of water was simply the straw that broke the camel's back. In any case, at 2:45 A.M. on the second day of the rain, approximately twenty-four hours before the time set for the break, a timber supporting the ceiling of Barrack III gave way with the resounding crack of a high-powered rifle. It hit the floor with a crash, fortunately not striking anyone. More loud noises followed as other ceiling beams broke under the added strain. The water-soaked earth started sliding slowly through the breaks, then faster, like an avalanche. Sleeping prisoners, deluged by the earth and struck by the beams, cried out in alarm and pain.

Mindful of their orders to ignore all suspicious activity, the guards restricted themselves to summoning Lieutenant Coleman, duty officer that night. As they waited, noises and yells echoed through the night. Lights went on in adjoining Barrack II. Cries for help rang out.

Breathless, Coleman arrived at the gate with the corporal of the guard and a squad of men. Deciding he could not pretend to ignore the obvious, yet fearing a ruse, Coleman ordered the searchlights in the towers turned on Barrack III. At the barred windows were some prisoners clamoring for help.

"Alert the camp," Coleman ordered the man nearest him. "The rest of you, follow me," he told the squad. "We're going in. This may be a real emergency in there, or it may be the break. If it is the break, they mean us to be sucked in, so play the game."

The corporal unlocked the gate and Coleman led them toward Barrack III on the double.

A light sleeper since the discovery of the escape plot, Gallant was awakened by the distant noises. He reached for the walkie-talkie beside his bed and contacted the perimeter guard.

"Anything stirring?"

"Nothing," each post reported in turn.

"There's something happening in camp," he warned them. "Don't know what it is yet. Stay on your toes."

Unbarring the door of Barrack III, Coleman and the corporal of the guard played the light of their torches inside, where some men were still trapped under mud and debris. Those who

hadn't been buried and had recovered their wits were attempt-
ing to aid their comrades. Others were stumbling about in the
darkness, adding to the confusion.

"Everyone outside!" Coleman shouted. "Outside, all of you
who aren't helping!"

Leaving two men to assemble the prisoners, Coleman led the
others inside. Arriving a few minutes later, Gallant found them
searching through the rubble for those who might be lying unconscious. Most of the prisoners had already streamed out of
the barrack, the able-bodied helping the injured. In their pajamas, they stood under the heavy rain, mud and water dripping
off them. Among them was Colonel Unger, his streaked face
wide-eyed in shock.

"Start moving these men up to the gymnasium," Gallant ordered a squad of reinforcements coming up on the scene. Recognizing Delamare among them, he added, "Stick around,
Del."

"They're all out," Coleman came to tell him.

"Good. Have a count made of them immediately. Lend me
your flashlight," he requested as Coleman turned to go.

"Did they break out?" Delamare asked.

"Not unless this is stage setting." He moved the light over the
wreckage.

Delamare turned his torch on the gaping hole in the ceiling.

"I'll have a look up there," the sergeant proposed and began
to pile footlockers one on top of another.

With Gallant bracing the improvised platform, Delamare
climbed to the top and flashed his light around the attic.

"Can you see the direction my light is pointed?" he called
down.

"Yes, toward the wardrobes."

"Take a fix on the exact one."

"Got it."

"That's where the tunnel entrance must be. There's a pulley here where they must have been hauling up the earth."

Delamare jumped down. Gallant opened the door to the closet he had spotted. He examined the paneling inside by the light of his torch. Delamare followed him in and rapped on the panels. They sounded solid.

"Must be in here," he muttered. "Does it matter if I rip the place up a bit?"

"Go ahead," Gallant said resignedly. "They're not going to be able to use it any more. We can't pretend we don't know where all this earth came from."

Delamare straight-legged his heavy boot into the end panel, splitting it. He pulled the broken boards away. Gallant's light revealed the shaft and the ladder fixed to the wall.

In the chamber below a mass of equipment, including the clandestine radio, disclosed why the last search of the barracks had drawn a blank.

"Some haul," Delamare commented. "This is going to put them out of business for a long time."

Gallant's light probed the tunnel. The beam failed to carry to the end.

"Let's see how far it goes," he suggested.

The two men crawled through the two-foot-high tunnel to the end.

"I make it about five hundred feet," Gallant gasped in the fetid atmosphere.

"About that." Delamare fingered the earth on the facing. It was dry. "Looks like they haven't been digging recently. This must be as far as they planned to go. They're way beyond the wall now."

"The escape could have been set for any day now, then," Gallant mused. "Damn!"

They turned and slithered back through the muddy tunnel.

Pragmatist that he was, Modersohn was already thinking in terms of his next move. News of the collapse had come to him almost immediately via his efficient grapevine. The inmates of Barrack II had seen enough of the disaster to be able to surmise what had happened. They conveyed the news to Barrack I through a side window.

Modersohn himself stood at the corresponding window reading their semaphore signals. Before the full description ended, he retired to sit in his wooden armchair at the head of the refectory table. The excited murmuring in the barrack ceased as the seventy-nine other men in the room conceded an atmosphere of privacy to their chief. Staring directly ahead, back straight, his hands whitening from their grip on the arms of the chair, Modersohn remained motionless for fifteen minutes. There was no necessity for split-second decision so the U-boat commander allowed himself the luxury of controlled anger. Unger served as his whipping boy. As engineering officer, the responsibility was his. That had to be made clear to Berlin.

Having found his scapegoat, Modersohn methodically turned his thoughts to recouping the situation for himself. His duty—and his reputation—was now in insuring the safety of the U-536 and the U-841. The U-boats were to linger off the coast for five days waiting for the escapees. Each night at the appointed hour they would run in at periscope depth to look for the signal. It would be subjecting them to unnecessary jeopardy to do this for nothing.

"Rednitz!" Modersohn's sharp voice broke the unnatural silence.

"Sir." Rednitz bounded to the table.

"You were working on a solitary escape plan before we started the tunnel, is that right?"

"Yes, sir."

"Could you put your plan into action immediately, leave to-morrow night?"

"Yes, sir," Rednitz replied without hesitation. "I need only a minimum of equipment, all of which is readily available."

"You will have all the assistance you need for your preparations. You will time your departure to meet Schmidt and Hochbauer at 01:30 hours. Your assignment is to inform the U-536 and the U-841 that they are not to wait for us. If Schmidt and Hochbauer fail to appear, you will proceed to the rendezvous alone."

Rednitz nodded his understanding.

"In such event, expedience will be your guide. The escape committee will give you travel information. The railroad will be your best method of transportation, but you will have to commandeer automobiles at the start and finish of the voyage. Arrange so that the owners cannot signal the fact.

"You will, of course, return to duty in the Fatherland with the rescue boats."

"Thank you, sir. I shall get through," Rednitz assured him.

CHAPTER 16

A pallid, exhausted Perry called Gallant to his office the following morning to ask wearily: "What now?" His nascent spirit of adventure dampened by another sleepless night, he longed for nothing more than to be told Bowmanville might return to its normal routine.

"Now we wait some more," Gallant answered grimly, also weary of the months of marking time which had ended in such a farcical climax.

"There are still Schmidt and Hochbauer," Gallant pointed out. "If they are in on this and Modersohn doesn't have a way of warning them, they may still lead us to the rendezvous."

"We just continue waiting then?"

"Perhaps it won't be long. The work in the tunnel was completed. They could have made their break any day."

Perry waved his hand dubiously.

"At least we know now where the tunnel exit is," Gallant extended a positive thought. "I'm concentrating our perimeter guard in that area. If Schmidt and Hochbauer come anywhere near there, we won't miss them."

Like athletes before a match, Schmidt and Hochbauer were getting plenty of rest that day, lying abed late, preparing for the long dash they were to make.

Both men had requested two days off from their jobs to account for their absence. Schmidt pretended that a buyer had turned up for the truck who required him to deliver it to Quebec. Leaving with the truck the evening before, he had garaged it near their home. Hochbauer claimed a family crisis.

Their landlady was treated to a different tale. To explain their midnight departure, they told her they were catching a night train for a few days' vacation.

Schmidt and Hochbauer collected the truck and the motorcycle and drove east out of Toronto at a sedate pace. It was still raining, and Hochbauer was wearing high rubber boots, a long yellow oilskin slicker and a fisherman's southwester. He preceded the truck by about a hundred yards, slowing occasionally to make sure it was following.

Twenty miles out of Toronto, Hochbauer, followed by Schmidt, turned off the highway into a deserted picnic area screened by trees.

Unlocking the tail gate, Schmidt climbed into the truck and passed four signboards down to Hochbauer. The two longer ones they bolted to the sides of the truck in places prepared for them. The shorter ones went in the front and rear. The job took only a few minutes. It changed the anonymous truck into a vehicle to be respected, a vehicle not to be approached. The signs read: "DANGER—HIGH EXPLOSIVES." At each corner of the truck they affixed a red flag to complete the disguise.

Without pausing to admire the effect, the two U-boat officers turned to their next chore. While Hochbauer busied himself in the body of the truck, Schmidt went to work on the motorcycle. A few minutes later Hochbauer emerged wearing the uniform of a Mounted Policeman and his machine bore the emblem of that organization.

Ten minutes after midnight, Modersohn ceremoniously shook hands with Rednitz. Not a word passed between them. Rednitz already had his instructions. There was no further need for talk.

Two officers removed the iron bars framing a window in the rear of Barrack I. They slid out of the stonework without difficulty. The passage had been used many times before. Rednitz swung himself over the ledge. Dressed in black trousers and a black turtleneck sweater, his face and hands were also tinted black. He carried a small canvas seabag and on his feet were heavy paratrooper's boots.

Rednitz dropped the few feet to the ground, landed silently, and stood motionless for a few seconds, looking to the left at the small section of the wall visible from that point. A guard walked by. Immediately after, Rednitz sprinted across the lighted area separating Barracks I and IV. The rain made his footing precarious.

Pressing close to the barrack wall, he edged his way toward the inner quadrangle formed by Barracks IV, V, VI, and VII, and the mess and recreation halls.

Inside the quadrangle he was partially hidden from the guards on the wall. He sprinted the length of Barrack IV, then stopped to look up and down the passageway. No guards were in sight. Rednitz dashed across and on, to the end of Barrack VI, where he again checked the wall. He ran across to the recreation hall and circled around it, moving in the narrow shadow cast by the eaves.

To the rear of the recreation hall lay the tennis courts. They offered no shadow, no protection from the floodlights on the walls. Tying the seabag around his neck, Rednitz got down on the ground and, moving at the pace of a snail, started the long crawl to his objective, five hundred feet away. He paused only at the trip wire to assure himself that the seabag slid under it without catching.

Thirty feet inside the forbidden zone delineated by the trip wire, Rednitz reached his objective: an electric line pole, a still functioning remnant of the original installation of the Bowmanville Reformatory.

Curled at the base of the pole, Rednitz opened the seabag and drew forth a set of primitive climbing spikes similar to those used by linemen. The spikes themselves had been extracted from the main joists of Barrack I. They were imbedded in an improvised harness of wood and leather which Rednitz fastened to his boots.

The seabag draped over his back, Rednitz drew himself erect against the pole. Embracing it with both arms, he cautiously sank first one spike, then the other into the soft wood. Slowly he let his weight rest on the spikes, testing to see if they held. The right spike slipped free, tearing a sliver out of the pole. Rednitz was thrown off balance. He clutched for support, drew himself upright on his left spike. It held. Raising his right leg, he drove the spike in at a wider angle this time, forcing it in by muscle power since he feared the noise of a sharp thrust.

In slow motion, taking tiny steps to keep his silhouette at one with the pole, Rednitz cramponned his way up.

On a level with the top of the wall he froze, sure that a guard looking in his direction saw him. After a few seconds, the guard turned away. Rednitz renewed his climb, more swiftly now that he was above eye level.

At the crosstrees, not pausing to rest, Rednitz shifted the seabag in front of him and drew out a bo's'n's chair rigged to a small trolley. The apparatus consisted of a pair of small wooden wheels with convex rims mounted on a single axle. Rednitz placed the wheels on the two parallel cables carried by the pole. The carpentry shop had judged accurately. The axle bridged the distance between the cables exactly. After fastening the rope from the seat to the axle, which had been left unattached, Rednitz hoisted himself into the chair. His movement had the grace of a professional acrobat.

A glance below to assure himself that none of the guards were gazing heavenward and Rednitz pushed off from the pole.

The wooden wheels turned stiffly on their improvised axle. The conveyance moved slowly down the inclined cable toward the next pole five hundred feet away. Passing over the wall, Rednitz looked smugly down at the guard almost directly below him.

Toward the halfway mark, the bo's'n's chair started to lose momentum. As the cable began to slant upward, with the wheels barely moving, Rednitz reached up to propel himself by hand.

With each foot the angle increased. The wheels turned more and more reluctantly, jamming frequently on their wooden axle. At one hundred fifty feet from the next pylon, the wheels froze. Tug as he might, Rednitz could only skid them forward an inch or two at a time. Swearing under his breath, he chinned himself on the wire with one hand, using the other to free the wheels. With his weight off them, they turned but as soon as he dropped back in the chair they blocked again.

Rednitz swung in the chair, his clothes as wet with sweat as with rain, and stared at the ground thirty feet below, pondering his problem with schooled calm.

He rubbed his hands together to restore their suppleness. Then, reaching up, he hoisted himself out of the chair and began swinging hand over hand along the cable. Each time he made contact with the cold, wet cable, Rednitz tested his grip, assuring himself he could hold before releasing the other hand and swinging on. The coarse strands of wire bit deeply into his palms. His movement set the cable dancing and swaying, challenging him to keep the rhythm or be bounced off.

With each fresh grip his hands grew increasingly numb. Rednitz clenched his teeth. He silently gave his hands the order for each movement.

"Hold. Release. Swing. Grab." And on to the next series. "Hold. Release. Swing. Grab."

The cable seemed to stretch without end. His hands wanted to stop, but they obeyed orders. At last he could see the crosstrees on the next pylon. Three more swings and he grasped the thick wooden pole, wrapping his legs, then his arms around it. He flexed his bleeding hands to restore the circulation to them.

After a few minutes' rest, Rednitz cautiously lowered himself down the pole, planting each spike firmly. He had seen films of Canadian lumberjacks scampering down towering firs and would have done likewise on a dare. But on a mission he was caution itself.

Once on the ground Rednitz hastened to rid himself of the clumsy spikes. As he unlaced the straps, he peered through the rainy blackness to try to spot any movement in the fields around him. The way seemed clear. He consulted his wristwatch: 01:23 hours. He was late. Schmidt and Hochbauer would arrive at the meeting place in seven minutes. Preferably, he was to be waiting for them.

Carrying the spikes, Rednitz set off at a lope, a pace he knew he could hold. He had a mile and a half to go, most of it through a wooded area. He had scouted part of the terrain while out on parole, but the paths were more difficult to follow at night and treacherously muddy after three days of rain.

Leaving the picnic grounds, Hochbauer had maintained a twenty-five-yard lead, riding the center of the road to force on-coming traffic well over to the right. There were few vehicles on the road to notice the small convoy, but after passing through the town of Bowmanville, the occupants of a sedan concealed along the side of the road remarked their passage.

"Sure as hell wouldn't like to be driving that damn thing," said the man behind the wheel.

"Wouldn't like to be on that bike either. He must be soaked through to his drawers," his companion replied, picking up a microphone.

"Hello, Car Two. Come in. Got one heading your way. An explosives truck with a motorcycle escort. Yeah, just one cycle. Yeah, I do, too. Wouldn't like to have any shooting while he's in the neighborhood. 1:25. Signing off."

Taking a clipboard from the side pocket, the radio man entered the passage of the truck and motorcycle on a ruled sheet of paper. Car Two, three miles north, sat waiting for the convoy to pass.

On the dot at 1:30, as if participating in an automobile rally, Schmidt and Hochbauer turned their vehicles off Highway 2 into a small glade. They maneuvered in a circle so as to park one alongside the other facing the highway. Both switched off their lights and motors and sat quietly listening to the night sounds.

Accustomed to the loneliness of a U-boat bridge, neither spoke as the minutes went by without a sign of any sort. Headlights showed down the road. Hochbauer got off his cycle.

Schmidt drew a blanket from the rack above his head and unfolded it on the seat. In the event of a curious patrol car, Hochbauer had been instructed to say that the driver of the explosives truck was too fatigued to continue and was taking a nap.

The car passed without noticing them. Hochbauer walked to the road and watched as its taillights disappeared. The rain continued unabated. Hochbauer stood sentinel in front of the truck, unmoving.

"Car Two to Car One," the radio crackled, "that truck and motorcycle haven't passed yet."

"Maybe they stopped to commune with nature," Car One replied, mindful of being on the air. "If they don't turn up in five minutes, we'll reconnoiter."

Well into the woods, Rednitz tossed the climbing spikes away without breaking his stride. By the time they were found he would be far away. He stopped only twice to make out the path and each time was off again in seconds.

Twelve minutes after leaving the pylon, Rednitz came to the highway directly opposite the clearing where his fellow officers were waiting. In the stillness of the night the thud of his boots on the concrete was distinct. Hochbauer moved warily to the side of the truck where he could not be seen immediately by someone coming from the highway. Schmidt grasped a jack handle. They were expecting twenty-six men, not one.

The running man emerged from the darkness and headed toward the truck without hesitation. Hochbauer recognized the squat figure.

"Rednitz?"

"Yes." He headed for the cab.

"The others?" Schmidt queried, opening the door.

"Not coming. Let's go." He threw himself onto the seat.

Obedience overpowering curiosity, Hochbauer sprang on his motorcycle and kicked the starting pedal. Schmidt touched the ignition and the GMC came to life. The motorcycle bounced over the rough terrain and, at the highway, turned east. Schmidt eased the truck forward slowly, gathered speed on the shoulder and angled onto the concrete. The empty truck picked up with almost the ease of a passenger car. Schmidt flashed his lights to indicate he was following without difficulty.

Two minutes later, at 1:37 according to its log sheet, Car Two called Car One: "Your high-explosives truck just rolled through. You can save yourselves the trip."

"Check," the operator in Car One replied. "Glad to have that out of the neighborhood."

Awake in his cot in Barrack I, Modersohn plotted the progress of Rednitz as he might have that of a U-boat creeping underwater through an enemy minefield. He visualized every step Rednitz had to take, every obstacle he had to overcome. His innate sense of time told him the passing hours without the necessity of referring to his watch.

It was almost as though he himself were making the escape, climbing the pylon, sliding along the cables, meeting Schmidt and Hochbauer, and exulting in the power of the truck as it sped its way toward the coast. He had been tempted to go in Rednitz's place, but his judgment had mastered that fantasy. Command was his proper function, not derring-do. Rednitz was the ideal man for the escape. Modersohn, despite his thirty-nine years, liked to think himself equal to any task, but he had to admit his former leutnant's physical superiority—to any man in camp, not only to himself.

At five in the morning, Modersohn willed himself to sleep. He had reviewed Operation Kiebitz and found that, despite its failure, it could redound to his credit. He had shown his mettle and his name had been kept in the limelight. Unger was the one who would have to pay the piper for the fiasco. Perhaps it was just as well, he rationalized, that he hadn't succeeded in his hazardous plan. The important thing was to survive this intermediate period. His destiny lay in the Germany that was to come, not in the debacle of Adolf Hitler.

Convoyed by Hochbauer in his uniform of authority, the truck with the ominous signs was abreast of the Thousand Islands resort area, rolling along Highway 2 at a steady forty miles an hour. On the opposite bank of the St. Lawrence lay the state of New York. The three-day rain had come to an end. Hochbauer, thoroughly chilled, looked to the first signs of dawn. He still had over eight hundred miles of the thousand-mile dash to cover.

CHAPTER 17

Were it not for a touch of lyricism that dwells in even the most mundane humans, Rednitz's flight might have gone unnoticed until roll call. Neglecting his duty for the space of a minute, a guard on the south wall turned his back on the monotony of the compound and marveled at the colors of the sunrise.

The only discordant note on the horizon was the power line, an intrusion of man on nature. He regarded it sourly, his eye running along the straight black lines of wire clashing with the soft roundness of the sky. He picked up the binoculars to make out an object that broke the pattern of the parallel cables, an object hanging from them.

"What do you make of that contraption?" He handed the

glasses to his companion in the tower. "Looks like a Rube Goldberg dohickey to me."

The other guard studied the dangling bo's'n's chair. He lowered the binoculars and followed the cable to the pylon inside the compound.

"If we're not a bunch of dumb bastards," he said, shaking his head as he reached for the phone.

"Corporal of the guard. Southeast tower reporting. I think there's been an escape. Yes. No, I don't know how many. You know that electric line that comes into camp? Yeah, well, some smart cookie did a high-wire act on it . . . with a kind of trolley. It's hanging there now."

Within a few minutes, Lieutenant Coleman, again pulling the duty watch, was in the tower while the corporal of the guard alerted Perry and Gallant. Before joining Coleman in the tower, the latter spoke to the perimeter guard, who said no one had passed through their sector and the radio cars which reported having checked out two suspicious vehicles.

"We've been looking at those goddamn poles for years," Coleman groaned, "and no one ever figured that one out."

"And I pulled in the perimeter guard," Gallant echoed as he turned to run down the stairs followed by Coleman. "They're all staked out around the tunnel, on the other side of camp.

"Get the ID parade going," Gallant ordered the puffing lieutenant. "And don't give them a chance to get out of the barracks or they'll be switching places again."

Finding Delamare at the gate with the troops forming to enter the compound, Gallant motioned the sergeant to join him. In a jeep, they skidded their way through the muddy fields to the electric line pylon outside the wall.

"Just one man," Delamare pronounced, reading the tracks in the mud without difficulty. "He came down the pole using climbing spurs." He pointed to the fresh scars in the wood.

"Think you can track him?"

"Should be able to in this mud."

Leaving the sergeant to follow the heavy boot prints left by the escaping prisoner, Gallant drove back to camp, where the guards, now fully assembled, were about to be marched into the compound by Howell and Coleman. Perry, his clothes disordered, was at the gate looking as though he needed to be given something to do.

"One man got away," Gallant informed them. "Colonel, can you please get things started in Ottawa? I'm going to run down to the highway to speak to the men in the patrol cars."

Relieved that only one and not twenty-eight of his charges had made away, Perry scuttled to his office. Gallant drove at breakneck speed over the muddy road to the highway, wanting to see for himself the list of the vehicles that had passed through the region that night.

"These are the only two that stopped, Captain." The driver of the radio car pointed to the entries on the ruled sheet of paper. "All the others buzzed through so fast you wouldn't know there's a speed limit.

"This one"—he put his finger on an entry at 24:03—"was an old man and his wife. We gave them five minutes like you said and then went up to investigate. The old boy was changing a tire while his wife was holding the light for him.

"Then there was this truck here at 1:25. It was a high-explosives truck, with a Mounted Policeman riding motorcycle escort in front of it. They were slow going through and we were just about to go up to have a look-see when the guys up in Car Two checked them out."

"You sure it was a Mounted Policeman? It was dark last night."

"He was riding in front of the truck, all lit up by its headlights. And the truck was lit up like a Christmas tree so you could see the signs on it, too."

"See what make it was?"

"No. It was a big one. Maybe ten tons."

The nearest telephone was in the all-night roadhouse a half mile down the highway in the direction of the camp. Gallant skidded the jeep to a halt directly in front of its door. He pulled a startled waitress out of the phone booth as she was composing a number.

"But my husband—I've got to get him up to go to work."

"He can have an extra fifteen minutes this morning, compliments of the army." Gallant slid the door closed.

Identifying himself to the sergeant on duty at Mounted Police headquarters in Toronto, Gallant requested:

"I want to know if you or any other MP post in the region assigned a man in uniform to ride motorcycle escort for a high-explosives truck. He passed through our sector at 1:30 this morning."

"I'll have to call you back, Captain," the MP said. "Can't give out information without being sure who we're talking to."

"Call back in five minutes!" Gallant snapped, reminded of former hassles with the federal police in covering news events. "I'm not calling from Bowmanville now, but I'll be there by then."

Modersohn came awake with full lucidity when the bolt on the barrack door was shot back. It was an hour before reveille. It could only mean that the escape had been discovered. He would know in a minute if Rednitz had been recaptured. If he was still at large, there would be an ID parade to determine who was missing. Unfortunately, there were no longer any effective measures to delay identification. Not since the new procedure.

"Everyone up!" Howell ordered from the doorway. "Fall in as you are for identification."

Modersohn smiled inwardly. The pajama-clad officers, stretching and cursing, lined up on one side of the dormitory.

his hand to stop them. Hochbauer nervously brought his machine to a halt, revving the motor to make sure of not stalling. Behind him the truck's airbrakes sighed. Two cars rattled off the bridge. The policeman waved them on.

In the communications room of the Royal Canadian Mounted Police headquarters in Ottawa, the phone call from the policeman at the first Valleyfield crossing was switched without delay to the office of Captain Caspery. It was the first report on the escaped prisoners since the alarm went out for them a little over two hours before.

"It's a ten-ton General Motors truck," the policeman reported precisely. "Painted gray, Ontario license number 947-470. Two men in the cab."

Caspery looked at his wall map to trace the routes open to the fugitives. A phone call from the officer on the third crossing cut down the possibilities. The fugitives had crossed the bridge on Highway 3, which they could either follow toward Montreal or leave in two and a half miles for Highway 36. After that, numerous secondary routes were open to them, west through the province of Quebec or south to the United States.

Giving his battery of telephone operators the new description of the truck, Caspery started them making a fanlike wave of calls to try to intercept the trio along any path they might take.

Twenty miles after turning onto Highway 36, the POWs made their first stop in almost nine hours since leaving the clearing outside of Bowmanville. They had maintained a steady speed over the traffic-less roads of thirty-five miles an hour. With over three hundred miles clocked off, Hochbauer's gasoline gauge was flickering toward zero. Spotting a thick grove of trees, he led the truck to concealment behind it.

Setting his emergency brake before the jeep was fully stopped in front of the administration building, Gallant jumped out of the rolling vehicle with a momentum that carried him bursting into the colonel's outer office.

"I'll take all phone calls in here," he told the flustered corporal.

The MP's call came through thirty seconds later while Gallant and Perry were exchanging information hurriedly. Perry's ordered sanctum took on the atmosphere of a front-line command post.

"Nobody has a man riding escort on an explosives truck, Captain," the police sergeant reported. "Shall I put out a pickup order for them?"

"Don't do a thing," Gallant told him. "It'll all be taken care of from Ottawa."

Jiggling the bar to get the attention of the operator, Gallant flashed a smile of thanks to Perry, who had passed the VIP ashtray to him.

"Brigadier Kerr in Ottawa," Gallant ordered. "His home number. Make it priority."

In a few seconds the connection was made. He spoke into the phone eagerly, delivering his message with telegraphic economy.

"Right," said Kerr as he finished.

The door opened and Howell erupted into the office.

"Can you hold on, Kerr? I'll have something more for you in a second."

"Right. I'll get Caspery on the other line."

Gallant lifted a questioning eyebrow at Howell.

"Rednitz," Howell said, trying to catch his breath, "Conrad Rednitz from Barrack I. Here."

He put Rednitz's ID photo and a card bearing his description on the desk. Gallant could hear Kerr speaking to Caspery on a second phone. He waited until Kerr brought the police captain up to date, then broke in, giving him a description of Rednitz. Kerr passed it on.

"Gallant"—he switched phones—"unless there's something more you can do down there, come on in. Caspery's got his telephone net set up. You can coordinate the operation better from his place."

"Right." Gallant caught himself using Kerr's phraseology. "I think I can make a plane out of Toronto that'll get me in faster than driving."

The phone rang as soon as Gallant replaced the receiver. He picked it up automatically, Perry standing by with not a look of protest at this breach of protocol. It was Delamare calling.

"I traced him to the highway," the sergeant recounted. "And then I thought I lost him until I saw some tire tracks coming out of a clearing on the other side. I picked up his prints again there. He seems to have joined up with what I guess is a truck. They were big tire prints. There were some motorcycle prints alongside. I'm pretty sure they were made at the same time."

"They were," Gallant told him. "The radio cars saw both of them.

"Del, do you know Conrad Rednitz by sight? He's the one you were tracking."

"I know him. Tough little character."

"Where are you calling from?"

"The roadhouse."

"Stay there. I'll pick you up in five minutes. You're flying to Ottawa with me. We might need someone who can identify Rednitz."

Five minutes after Gallant and Delamare boarded the 9:30-A.M. plane for Ottawa, a policeman on duty at the Valleyfield crossing of the St. Lawrence River, about thirty miles west of

Montreal, gave a go-ahead signal to an MP on a motorcycle and the high-explosives truck following him. Schmidt grinned and flicked his hand as if to thank the officer.

"This was a wonderful idea the fregattenkapitän had," he said to Rednitz. "We get treated like royalty with these signs on the truck."

No traffic was coming from the opposite direction. The two vehicles crossed the narrow span slowly as befitted the truck's supposed cargo. The patrolman on the bridge watched them until they were out of sight, then hobbled off on aching feet toward a gasoline station a half a mile away. The nearest telephone was located there.

Hochbauer shifted uneasily on the huge Harley-Davidson saddle, looking back at Schmidt and Rednitz. This was the section of the journey he feared most. His supremacy on a motorcycle was of little advantage here. The Valleyfield crossing consisted of three bridges traversing two islands. It was a natural trap where they could be bottled up if there was an alarm out for them. Modersohn had selected the route because he considered it the most expedient for them. Otherwise, they would have had to pass through the city of Montreal or make a time-consuming detour to the north. The crossings before Valleyfield were entirely out of the question. They led directly into the United States.

Two bridges crossed from the smaller island, on which they found themselves, to the larger one, where the town of Valleyfield was located. Hochbauer's instructions were to turn le[f]t and take the east bridge, which avoided the town. He half-sto[od] in the saddle at the approach to the bridge. It looked deserte[d]. He waved the truck on.

They crossed the bridge and moved onto the larger isla[nd]. Running down its length, they came to the third cross[ing] which would bring them to the mainland. A policeman hel[d]

Rednitz hopped out of the cab of the truck with a jerrycan. He filled the tank of the motorcycle while Hochbauer stiffly got off the machine and disappeared behind a tree. A shouted conversation apprised him of the failure of the mass break.

Schmidt's first concern during the stop was to walk critically around his huge truck, examining the tires and peering underneath to assure himself all was in order. Then he attended to his own needs and climbed back behind the wheel again. Rednitz took his place beside him.

Hastily gulping some coffee from a thermos carried in his saddlebag, Hochbauer straddled his machine. Replacing the thermos, he took out another of the sandwiches with which he had been sustaining himself while driving and signaled to his companions that he was prepared to start.

Not a car had passed to disturb their brief halt. The three men set out again, their confidence high as the sun which had broken through that morning.

Gallant studied the map on the wall of Caspery's office for what seemed the hundredth time. He had memorized the name of every hamlet and road the trio of Germans could be passing. It was over two hours since they had been sighted at Valleyfield and no word had been had of them after that.

"They must be sticking to the secondary roads," Caspery gave his opinion. "They could get through some of these villages without being noticed. Most of them have one-man police forces. They can't be everywhere at once."

Delamare stared out of the window, feeling out of place in this mechanical hunt.

A half hour later a call came in from Drummondville, about a hundred miles northeast of Valleyfield, reporting that the explosives truck had just passed through.

"Looks like they're staying in Canada." The police captain

consulted his map. "If they were headed for Vermont or Maine, they wouldn't have veered up north that way. They're on a course for the Gaspé now."

Reports coming in, although irregular, showed the fleeing Germans to be holding their course. At a monotonous thirty-five miles an hour, they were rolling up the center of the narrow stretch of Quebec province between the St. Lawrence and the Maine border.

As he had been doing regularly, Gallant called MacLevy to confirm that they were still heading in the direction of the Gaspé Peninsula. They could turn east into New Brunswick, of course, once north of the state of Maine.

"May I tell the Americans to call off the alert for their units off the Maine coast?" the navy commander inquired.

"Keep them on the hook another few hours," Gallant replied prudently. "It looks improbable, but they could still make a run for the Maine coast."

By five in the afternoon, it appeared extremely unlikely that they were planning to head into Maine and Gallant told Mac-Levy to advise the Americans to that effect. The POWs had been sighted joining up with Highway 2 once more, north of the city of Quebec.

Caspery phoned ahead to his posts on the highway and calls came in steadily as they followed that main artery northward.

"We're boxing them in now," Caspery noted with satisfaction. "They've got to stick on 2. The secondary roads up in this place won't take them anyplace.

"Here is their next choice." He indicated the junction between Highways 2 and 10 at Rivière du Loup, a hundred and twenty miles from Quebec. "We've got to spot them there."

Gallant glanced up from some calculations he was making on a slip of paper.

"They're traveling faster now that they're on the highway, averaging over forty miles an hour."

In the dusk, about two hours after bypassing Quebec, Hochbauer guided the truck off the highway. They parked behind a sheltering stand of pine. The area was uninhabited for miles around and traffic infrequent on the highway.

Despite their weariness after seventeen hours of nonstop driving, the three men fell immediately to their scheduled task. Schmidt and Rednitz unbolted the signs fixed to the truck while Hochbauer took off his uniform and donned heavy civilian clothing. He gratefully pulled on a sheepskin-lined leather jacket. The mid-September night was turning cold.

The switch was a last-minute order from Modersohn to Rednitz. The labeling of the truck and its uniformed outrider had been envisaged to forestall being stopped or searched while transporting a hidden cargo of prisoners. It was not particularly necessary for three men carrying impeccable identity papers. However, Modersohn had judged it still worthwhile for their journey through the relatively populated regions. Once beyond these, they could make better time and be less conspicuous without the high-explosives signs. As a precaution, Hochbauer was now to ride three miles in advance of the truck. In case of a road block he could speed back to warn his comrades.

Their vehicles transformed, they themselves somewhat rested and restored by food and drink, the three set out at a faster pace, no longer having to maintain the fiction of transporting explosives. Leaving three minutes before the truck, Hochbauer cruised steadily for three minutes at sixty miles an hour, then slowed to fifty. Schmidt maintained a steady fifty.

Looking for something as obvious as an MP on a motorcycle convoying an explosives truck, the watchers on Highway 2 failed to make the connection between the civilian on the motorcycle and the unmarked truck which passed three minutes later. In the dark, the truck's dust-covered license plate could not be read.

Over an hour ticked by without the phone in Caspery's office ringing. After the two previous hours of clockwork reports, the change was all the more puzzling.

"They could have stopped for dinner," Delamare suggested, chewing on a sandwich fetched from a nearby restaurant.

"Or for the night," Caspery added. "They must be worn out by now."

Impatiently, Gallant threw the sandwich he had picked up back onto the tray.

"If they stopped, it's not because they're worn out. They're keyed up, running free and homeward bound. That can sustain them without sleep for days."

Two MP's in a radio-equipped car hidden behind the bushes at the junction of Highways 2 and 10 at Rivière du Loup heard the deep roar of a motorcycle and saw its single head-light a few seconds before it came into view. It was 8:20 P.M., approximately the time the three Germans were expected to pass their station. They hunched themselves forward closer to the windshield. The motorcyclist swept into view, banked sharply as he took the right-hand turn without slowing down, and made off in the direction of Edmundston.

"False alarm," said the man behind the wheel.

"Yeah, he's traveling alone. So damn dark you can hardly see. But he wasn't wearing a uniform, was he?"

"Nah, didn't have a hat on."

Three minutes later headlights glimmered in the distance. As they came nearer, the two experienced patrolmen could tell from their height they were those of a large truck. It braked as it came to the juncture.

"What do you think?"

"It's a GMC ten-ton or I'll eat my hat."

"Yeah. But there are no high-explosives signs on it."

"Let's call it in anyway. Can't go wrong that way."

At a few minutes to nine the town of Cabano, thirty-two miles from Rivière du Loup on Highway 2, had already pulled in its sidewalks for the night. When a motorcyclist buzzed its main street, the shop windows were dark. The infrequent street lights were not bright enough to disturb the couple his beam illuminated, embracing in a parked car. Toward the end of the main street, a man was changing a tire in the light of a powerful electric lantern. When a heavy truck pounded through town three minutes later, the man crouching beside the wheel was able to read the number of its license plate in the light of the lantern.

"It's them all right," Caspery said, replacing the receiver.

He joined Gallant and Delamare in studying the wall map. Cabano was twenty-four miles from the border of the province of New Brunswick, thirty-five miles from the city of Edmundston. And from Edmundston to the sea at its nearest point, Campbellton, at the start of Chaleur Bay, was one hundred twenty-eight miles.

Caspery and Gallant each took a phone.

"Commander MacLevy, please," Gallant said after dialing.

"Tell Edmundston they'll be passing through in about three-quarters of an hour," Caspery ordered a switchboard man. "And get me the post at St. Leonard. I'll speak to them in person."

"We'll know as soon as they get to St. Leonard if they're heading up toward Chaleur Bay or if they're continuing on south," Gallant was saying to MacLevy. "They should be in St. Leonard in less than an hour and a half at the rate they're traveling."

"That would put them in Campbellton in two and a half hours, then." MacLevy consulted his own map.

"Do you have any units there?"

"We can get them there but no submarine is going to come in as far as Campbellton. If they're going to meet in the bay, it'll more likely be somewhere out near the mouth. And, as you know, they could swing down the coast and join up on the ocean front. You'll have to be breathing down their necks from now on. We've got a fair number of ships in the area, but you've got to give us time to pinpoint them."

"What if they don't head up that way? If they keep on going south to Fundy?"

"It'll give us more time to get set up if they do. That's a long drive. We can count on support from the U.S. down there, too."

"Draft somebody if you have to." Gallant overheard Caspery speaking to the post in St. Leonard as he hung up on MacLevy. "I don't care about your personnel problems. I want three observation posts set up. One at the junction, one to the east to cover that cutoff on 17, and one to the south for extra security."

As precisely now as if running on a franchised schedule, the motorcycle and the truck passed through the checkpoints established by Caspery. Edmundston telephoned word of their passage at 9:45 P.M. During the half hour after that, reports came in from five villages on Highway 2, which at that point runs along the St. John River directly across from Maine.

At 10:25, Hochbauer was observed at the junction in St. Leonard where he turned left on Highway 17. The truck followed in his path three minutes later. The car at the cutoff five miles east of town, where they might have turned to rejoin Highway 2 further south, radioed that they continued straight on. The car was told to remain in position. If the Germans were feinting to throw off possible pursuers, they wouldn't be able to backtrack without being spotted.

The next town on Highway 17, St. Quentin, as well as each town beyond it, was taken off standby status and put on alert. St. Quentin lies forty-one miles from St. Leonard. In between is an unbroken stretch of country, almost completely uninhabited, where it hadn't been thought necessary to station watchers.

An hour and a half had gone by without news although the Germans should have reached St. Quentin in under an hour.

"St. Quentin calling," the switchboard operator announced to Caspery. A frown appeared on Caspery's face as he listened to the message. Gallant and Delamare looked at him anxiously.

"No, I'll notify you if we do hear anything," Caspery spoke into the telephone gruffly. "You keep your men at their posts until I tell you to take them off. They must have stopped for a while.

"No news," he said to his two army visitors as he dropped the phone into place.

"Midnight." Gallant looked at his watch. "They don't seem to be in a hurry any more."

"Maybe the rendezvous isn't for tonight," Caspery suggested.

"Could be they're lying low till the last minute," Delamare observed. "Might not want to take a chance being seen hanging around the coast."

Caspery opened his tie and propped his feet on the desk.

"It's going to be a long night. I'm going to get some shut-eye. There are some cots in the next office, if you want."

"Thanks." Gallant flexed his neck as he stood up.

"They can't go anywhere," Delamare said confidentially as he started for the door. He had hunted throughout the area and knew its inaccessibility. There was no possibility for the Germans to leave 17. No roads intersected it and the country was too rough to cross. The nearest parallel road lay almost a hundred miles to the south.

Accustomed to snatching rest during periods of stress, the three U-boat skippers lay asleep on air mattresses in the roomy body of the GMC. Well concealed from the road, the vehicle was parked near one of the numerous rivers of New Brunswick. They had stopped for the night at 11 o'clock, midway between St. Leonard and St. Quentin, congratulating themselves on the ease of their journey.

"A shame the rendezvous wasn't set for tonight," said Hochbauer, kindling a fire for their meal. "We could have made it. All we had to do was drive faster."

"And if we had a few flat tires?" Schmidt reprimanded him. "The boats would be sitting out there for nothing."

Rednitz undressed and washed himself in the icy river.

"Come on in. Condition yourselves. We may have to swim tomorrow night. If there's an emergency, there won't be time to wait for the dinghy."

Lying awake restlessly, impatient for the day to begin, Gallant threw off his blanket and swung his feet to the floor when he heard the phone ring in the adjoining office. Delamare opened his eyes. Instantly alert, he lay without moving, straining to hear. Only a few muffled words came to him, then the bang of a receiver being dropped. Delamare jumped out of bed and reached for his shoes. Gallant was tying his laces.

"They're on the move." Caspery stuck his head in the door. "Just went through St. Quentin."

It was 6:30 in the morning. September twelfth. The three Canadians in their sleep-rumpled clothing distractedly gulped tepid coffee as they waited for the next call. It came exactly eleven minutes after the first, from the town of Kedgwick, ten miles down the line.

"They're not dragging their feet," Caspery commented. "They'll be smelling salt water in an hour. I wouldn't put it past them to shove off in daylight despite what MacLevy says. It would be unexpected. That would reduce the risk some."

"Unless they have a particular reason for it, there'd be no

point in taking the chance. The odds are MacLevy is right," Gallant answered.

He rubbed his hand over the stubble on his face.

"Anyway, while I can I'm going to have a wash. Del, I have an extra shirt and things. No use our feeling like escaped prisoners."

The escaped prisoners, freshly groomed after the icy early-morning bath instigated by Rednitz, continued their supervised route, turning right on Highway Eleven at the town of Tide-head to follow the south shore of Chaleur Bay.

MacLevy, who had put in an early-morning appearance at Mounted Police headquarters, oriented his naval forces toward that coast. Not having chosen the easy way around to the north shore via Matapédia at the head of the bay, there was little likelihood that the fugitives would take one of the ferry crossings.

With the meticulousness generally ascribed to Germans, the POWs arrived at the city of Campbellton precisely at the hour the men following their progress from Ottawa, six hundred miles away, were able to forecast. At this point, a backup car joined the cavalcade. The car was to follow a few minutes behind the truck. Its purpose was to note the point, presumably that of the rendezvous, where the truck eventually would pull off the road. The Campbellton backup car was an unmarked private sedan. Unfortunately, no two-way radio sets were available to equip all the backup cars which were standing by.

From Campbellton, the Germans' steady fifty miles an hour carried them the seventeen miles to Dalhousie in a little over twenty minutes. The Dalhousie post of the RCMP checked Hochbauer through at 8:10 A.M., Schmidt and Rednitz a few minutes later.

A few blocks from where he was sighted leaving Dalhousie,

Hochbauer had to take violent evasive action to avoid two dogs. There being no room to swing around the animals, Hochbauer threw his machine into a broadside skid. The dogs scooted across the road. Hochbauer's rear wheel hit a puddle. Unnoticed by him, some muddy water splashed a middle-aged woman who was window-shopping on the sidewalk.

Skillfully righting his heavy cycle, Hochbauer shifted into first gear and was about to resume his journey when, shrieking, the woman clutched at his arm.

"My dress, my dress!" she screamed. "You've ruined it!"

Rejecting the temptation of flight for so trivial a reason, Hochbauer attempted to speak to the woman. Encouraged, she shouted all the more hysterically. Several persons ran out of the two shops in front of which the incident had occurred and gathered around the motorcycle.

"Look at it! Look at my dress!" the woman repeated endlessly.

Hochbauer drew some money from his pocket.

"I'll pay for it." He looked righteously at the spectators.

"And my ankle. I turned my ankle on account of him."

Hochbauer tried unsuccessfully to get a word in edgewise.

"Are you insured? Where's your insurance?" the woman, now hobbling on one leg, yelled. "You see! He has no insurance."

"Here." Hochbauer thrust some money at her and tried to disengage himself from the small crowd surrounding him.

The woman's shrieks rose to a crescendo.

A uniformed figure, a local policeman on his way to work, loomed up in front of Hochbauer. He listened helplessly to the ranting of the woman and decided: "We'll straighten this out at the station."

Schmidt and Rednitz came on the scene to see Hochbauer being led away by a policeman, a wildly gesticulating female at their side.

"Keep going," Rednitz warned.

Schmidt had no intention of stopping. Their orders covered such an eventuality. Anyone in trouble was to be left.

"Maybe it has nothing to do with us," he said hopefully, then shook his head ruefully. "That Hochbauer! I wonder why the woman was shouting at him?"

Backing them up by a few minutes, the Campbellton car passed Hochbauer, the policeman, and the woman while they were hidden from the road by a parked trailer truck. The small crowd that had gathered was still grouped around the Harley-Davidson, obscuring it from sight as well.

"Charlie Station reporting," Caspery heard as he answered the call from the town ten miles south of Dalhousie. "The truck just went by but there's no sign of the motorcycle."

"How many men in the truck?"

"Two."

"Call me back right away if the motorcycle turns up."

Immediately placing a call to Dalhousie, Caspery ordered that RCMP post to send an unmarked car out to look for the missing motorcyclist.

The Dalhousie man stuttered: "I—I think we have your man here in the building. I mean the local police have him in their side of the building."

"What!" Caspery roared.

"They just brought in a motorcyclist on the complaint of some woman, an accident or something. She's been yelling like a banshee for five minutes."

"And you just sat there doing nothing?"

"I—I didn't know it was him."

"You had his description. The local police should have had it, too. What's the charge against him?"

"I don't think there'll be one. Looks like he just splashed some mud on her."

"Well, call your local guy aside and get him to say it was all a mistake. But do it fast and get him out of there."

Indignant and furious, Hochbauer never doubted the reason for his sudden release. He had shown his papers, which were all in order, and had defended himself eloquently against the either demented or calculating female. As much in a rush to leave as the police were to have him do so, he accepted their apologies and hastened back to his motorcycle. He had lost twenty-five minutes.

With the truck ahead of him, Hochbauer had a legitimate excuse for speed. Not concerned about the police on the little-traveled New Brunswick highway, Hochbauer at last took his pleasure in letting the Harley out. Opening up the engine which he had lovingly souped up, Hochbauer flattened himself over the handlebars, racing at almost twice the speed of the truck. He went by the nondescript sedan trailing the truck at a clip that precluded his noticing its make or occupants. Hochbauer had eyes only for the road. A pothole could be fatal.

"He'll kill himself and maybe others with him." Caspery ground his teeth as telephone messages, one on top of the other, attested to Hochbauer's race. "I should have left him in jail."

At Chaleur Beach, fifty-two miles from Dalhousie, Hochbauer overtook the comparatively lumbering GMC. Exhilarated, he waved in passing, signaling that all was well. One mile more and they entered Bathurst.

All four men in Caspery's office evidenced their anxiety as the call from the Bathurst MP post came in. Bathurst was a turning point. It would mean the end of the chase was near if the fugitives stayed on Highway 11, which would take them either to the mouth of Chaleur Bay or around the coast to one of the beaches on the open ocean. The other road from Bathurst, Highway 8, cut across the cape and would take them due south to Miramichi Bay or below.

"They're on 11," Caspery told them in an aside as he listened to the Bathurst MP.

MacLevy picked up a phone to call the naval transmitter.

Gallant dialed Kerr's number on another instrument, saying to Caspery as he did so: "Ask Bathurst if their airstrip is usable."

"It's a bit soft," Caspery was told. "We got the tail end of the hurricane. But we had a plane set down this morning and he's in one piece."

Caspery passed the information on to Gallant while the latter spoke to Kerr. A fourth telephone in the emergency installation rang. Delamare answered.

"Yes, Colonel. He's on another line. Yes, they're at Chaleur Bay now. Yes."

"Kerr, can you have a plane ready for me within an hour? They're probably going to wait around for dark. I can be down there long before then. I'll need something that can get into the Bathurst airstrip. Or, maybe worse, on the Atlantic coast."

"I was about to suggest that myself," Kerr answered. "Maybe being down there you can keep those imbeciles in line. Someone is bound to get butterflies at deadline. We can't afford another Hochbauer incident."

"Tell them to heave to between Miscou and Shippigan," MacLevy was saying. "From there they can go either way."

"If they park out that way," Caspery ordered, "get some men on the beaches to either side of them, but well out of sight. And have them stop any rubbernecks straying through."

"Colonel Perry for you." Delamare held his hand over the mouthpiece. "Wants to know if he can transfer Modersohn. There's a shipment going out to Camp Seebe in Alberta."

"Hello, Colonel. Yes, no objections. I'll call you as soon as we wrap it up."

Two Bathurst MPs in another radioless private car replaced the duo from Campbellton in trailing the convoy out on the cape. At Salmon Beach, a mile out of Bathurst, they were waved down by the man on lookout.

"Speed it up. They're way ahead of you."

The driver put the accelerator to the floorboard and held it there. Scanning both sides of the road for signs of the vehicles they were following, they pulled into sight of Schmidt's truck several seconds before they noticed it. The driver braked hastily to allow the truck to regain its lead.

At Janeville, six miles farther, the car was waved on by a patrolman at the school intersection. For another twelve miles, the three vehicles held their respective distances until the police car stopped at the fork where Highway 11 swings south and a regional road continues east to the town of Maisonette at the tip of the point. A man appeared from out of the brush.

"On out the point!" he yelled.

The road paralleled the edge of a cliff, thirty feet away. Both patrolmen knew it well. Not even a beach shack broke the wilderness for the next five miles. Here and there infrequently used footpaths led down the two-hundred-foot cliffs to the beaches below. Somewhere on that stretch of road the Germans would be ending their voyage.

"Car coming," warned Schmidt, standing high on the running board.

The truck was parked on the cliff side of the road, the motorcycle next to it, without any attempt at concealment. Hochbauer and Rednitz, who had been about to open the rear doors of the truck, turned and walked toward some bushes as though on a not unusual roadside occupation.

A ten-year-old Ford coupe passed at a conservative thirty-five miles an hour. The two men inside hardly glanced at the parked truck. Schmidt kept his eye on the car as it continued on toward Maisonette, two miles away. When it disappeared, he motioned to his companions. Hochbauer and Rednitz hastened to open the rear doors and unload a carton of food and drink and another of blankets. With Schmidt still acting as sentry, the two other men carried the cartons to the edge of the cliff, where they concealed them under a clump of the heavy brush covering the area.

Without a word, Rednitz crawled under the brush and settled himself on the ground as Hochbauer turned to leave. Schmidt was starting the engine of the GMC. He made a U-turn.

Returning circuitously through the woods on the opposite side of the road, one of the two occupants of the old Ford coupe stopped behind a tree as he came into sight of the spot. He saw the rear of the truck as it headed back down the road. A few seconds later, Hochbauer, whom he'd observed near the cliff, jumped on his motorcycle and roared off after the truck. The MP stood dumb struck, presuming all three Germans to have departed. He turned and ran through the woods, taking a shortcut to Maisonette, where his partner had gone to report the halt.

The first call from Maisonette came through to Bathurst at 10:20 A.M. Bathurst immediately called Ottawa and the machinery started rolling.

MacLevy ordered the corvette *Camrose* and the frigate *St. Catherine,* both lying between Miscou and Shippigan islands, twenty miles east of Maisonette, to take up positions behind Pokesudie Island, ten miles east of the spot where the Germans were reported. The commander likewise started other units converging on the area and directed the Sunderland bombers on coastal patrol to be within reach.

Caspery arranged for MP reinforcements to be rushed to Maisonette Point. Gallant and Delamare had a plane standing by and were on the point of leaving when the second call from

Maisonette via Bathurst came through. It started a fevered series of calls to the towns on the only two roads the Germans could take aside from the one leading to Bathurst. Both roads ran to the Atlantic coast.

Schmidt and Hochbauer drove without haste on the road back to Bathurst. They arrived there twenty minutes after the exhausted MP had come running into Maisonette with word of their departure. A policeman on duty at a crossing just inside the Bathurst city limits noticed their return. He had not yet heard that the Germans were on the move again but he had been among those assigned to spot them on the way out.

Schmidt drove his truck into the first service station in Bathurst, three blocks from where the policeman was stationed.

"Got room for me to park my truck here for a day or so?" he asked. "I'm waiting for a cargo."

"Put it in the back." The attendant pointed to the rear of the station.

Modersohn had thought of everything, Schmidt marveled, seeing the man go on about his work. The truck was too large to be hidden at the rendezvous. What better place for it than a garage in the nearest city?

After double-checking the locks on the truck, Schmidt walked to the corner where Hochbauer was waiting. He climbed onto the motorcycle and held fast to the saddle although Hochbauer drove slowly away from the curb. Once again heading for Maisonette, the two passed the policeman, who, after waiting to observe Schmidt's maneuvers with the truck, was making for the nearest phone.

Immediately after his call came into headquarters, other spotters on Highway 11 started reporting the motorcycle beelining for the point.

The news set Gallant, accompanied by Delamare, on a dash for the waiting plane. It was 11:30 A.M. They could be in Bathurst by midafternoon and, as Kerr put it, "wrap up their own story."

Operation Kiebitz was being wrapped up in Bowmanville as well. Fregattenkapitän Modersohn was told to make his preparations to leave for another camp in the morning. There was little for him to do. For the record, he officially handed over the control of the Lorient Group to Kapitänleutnant Kuhn. But the Lorient Group was considered by Berlin to be burned. It was on the inactive list of espionage rings since its supply of periodicals had been cut off. Apart from that, Modersohn had one other piece of unfinished business.

Unger.

On orders, Unger awaited the fregattenkapitän's pleasure, in the gymnasium, where, with the other men from Barrack III, he was quartered temporarily. Barrack III was uninhabitable. The tunnel had been sealed by dynamiting and its entrance plugged with concrete but repairs to the barrack awaited the arrival of new ceiling beams.

The engineering officer was sitting on his cot, his pen to his lips, unsuccessfully trying to express himself in a letter to his wife. He looked up to find Modersohn standing above him. Von Sperle and a young U-boat leutnant whom he knew only by sight were at the foot of his bed.

"Come," said Silent Willi.

Without looking back he walked to the steep steel staircase leading to the overhead running track which ovaled around the gymnasium. Unger followed. Von Sperle and the young leutnant brought up the rear.

Modersohn placed both hands on the railing of the track and looked below. The few officers who had been indoors that sunny morning were leaving. He turned to face Unger, staring stonily into his eyes.

"You are derelict in your honor," he said. "Normally, I should leave you with a loaded pistol. Unfortunately, we do not have this privilege."

Unger's face expressed the protest which his tongue was unable to form. Modersohn nodded over his head to Von Sperle. Unger jerked his head around.

Von Sperle's arm was out, extending a rope to him, a noose ready in one hand, the other end tied to the railing.

"No!" Unger gasped. "It wasn't my fault . . . the rain . . ."

"It was your responsibility." Modersohn walked around him to the staircase.

Unger tried to follow. Von Sperle and the leutnant blocked the narrow track. Modersohn left the building.

Near noon, after Unger was found dangling from the track railing, the letter he was writing to his wife was brought to Colonel Perry. "My darling wife," he had written. "I cannot say what is in my heart and perhaps you shall never, never know. . . ."

It could have been the beginning of a suicide note. Perry folded it sadly.

Modersohn systematically packed his personal belongings. Every object had its place, fitted neatly into its niche. Nothing would be left behind by error. Bowmanville was a closed chapter, neatly ended by the note he had read while looking over Unger's shoulder.

CHAPTER 18

"Any sign of life over there, André?" the MP sergeant from Bathurst whispered as he crawled up to the man lying under the scrub brush well back from the shoulder of the road.

The man called André shook his head and turned to look at the two strangers who were crawling behind the sergeant.

"Captain Gallant and Sergeant Delamare. Army. They're in charge here now."

André grunted a welcome.

"You sure they're in there?" Gallant peered across at the heavy bushes on the cliff side of the road.

"Haven't seen them, but here's where the truck was parked. And the guy on the motorcycle was messing around just over there when we first spotted him. Could have the motorcycle hidden over there, too, those bushes are so thick. Wasn't anything, not even a track we could see by the time we got here. Didn't want to follow them too close."

"Checked the beach?" Gallant asked. "They might be down there."

"No way of getting close enough."

"Boat," Gallant suggested. "Trawler or something that looks like it belongs. Have it stand off fairly far and examine the beach through glasses."

"Might get a trawler over at Maisonette," the sergeant said doubtfully.

"Trochot's sport fisherman's in. Saw it this morning," André whispered. "Got a ship-to-shore and twin Chryslers. Can move if he has to."

"Send your car," Gallant instructed the MP. "Have Trochot stay down the coast till tomorrow. Don't want him seen circling back."

The sergeant went back into the woods to use a walkie-talkie, one of several Gallant had distributed among the men staked out in the area.

Trochot's message was relayed back immediately after he cruised by the beach at Maisonette Point. No one to be seen, neither on the beach nor on the cliff above.

"They've got to be in there," the MP sergeant insisted. "No way for them to get by us unless they swam."

Gallant propped himself on his elbows to scan the landscape for the hundredth time. The late-afternoon sun was down. A faint wind ruffled some of the higher bushes. Otherwise all was motionless. He turned on his side, suppressing a cough. The ground was hard and damp under him. No more so, he consoled himself, than for the three presumably on the other side of the road.

Presumably. The hours dragged by and not the slightest stir indicated whether they were there or not. From time to time, one of the four Canadians glided back into the woods to puff a cigarette or hastily swallow a sandwich and some coffee. The Germans, if they were there, seemed to be in total hibernation until, at 9:30, Delamare whispered: "Hear that?"

"What?"

"A clink. Like glass."

"Didn't hear anything," the MP sergeant said.

"Me neither," André cast his doubt.

It was Delamare again who saw the first cautious figure rising from the brush in the light of the half-moon at eleven o'clock. Putting a warning hand on Gallant's arm, he pointed. Two other figures appeared. The three made their way to the edge of the cliff and, like phantoms, one by one slowly sank from sight over the side.

Gallant stood up, the others joining him.

"Del, get down on the beach to the left. Call if you see them signaling or the U-boats coming in. Don't let any of the men down there close in until I say so. I'll be on the right.

"Sergeant, André, cover the path they just used. Is there any other way for them to get back up?"

"No."

"Okay, then bring the men up on top here in a bit closer. And if you see anything at all, call. You should see the U-boats first from up here.

"All of you, in case we lose contact, no one is to show himself under any circumstance until the U-boats are under attack. They'll dive at any sign of trouble."

Soft, miniature waves uncurled their tongues caressingly on the sand at the feet of the three U-boat skippers. The waters of the bay lay calm, without even a swell. Except for the moonlight, which sent diamonds flickering on the black surface of the water, the feathering wake of a periscope would be easy to see. As their watches advanced toward the appointed moment, they scanned the bay without reward.

Using a compass, Schmidt aligned the long barrel of a six-cell flashlight directly to the northeast. The lens of the light bore a black mask with a tiny cross cut out in the center. Hochbauer and Rednitz stood on either side of him, holding their watches to catch the moonlight. Precisely at 1:15 A.M. they both hissed an urgent "Now!"

Schmidt's thumb pressed the button switch: two shorts, one long, three shorts, one long, one short.

They waited.

To their right, on an oblique line, Gallant was the first to catch sight of the flashes. He brought his walkie-talkie to his car and called the radio-equipped car on the highway above. His message was heard as well on the other walkie-talkies.

"They're signaling from the beach. Tell the navy to stand by."

The radio car shortwaved the message.

Anchor chains sent their rattlings echoing through the hulls of the corvette *Camrose* and the frigate *St. Catherine* as they prepared to stand to sea. Their engines turned slowly to hold them in place against the tide, awaiting the moment that the U-boats were sighted and they could slip out from between the islands. To do so before might give the show away in the event the U-boats were late to the rendezvous.

Patrolling Chaleur Bay, to the west, the destroyer *Chaudière* sounded action stations and held her place beyond sight.

Overhead, two Sunderlands circled out of hearing distance.

Time playing havoc with their senses after one minute elapsed, the three Germans glanced constantly from their watches to the water. The next four minutes seemed not to want to pass. They were to repeat the signal in five minutes if their rescuers did not appear.

Two hundred feet above them, the trooper André pointed out the form of a conning tower emerging from the sea a half mile out. His sergeant whispered the sighting into his walkie-talkie. A few seconds later Hochbauer jubilantly made the discovery. And in another thirty seconds both sides saw the second conning tower break water.

At reduced speed, the two U-boats crept in toward the unknown coast. On deck, their crews moved purposefully, preparing to launch inflatable rubber boats. The gun crews fed shells into the twin 2-cm. machine guns in the turret they called the "upper winter garden" and into the 3.7 in the lower winter garden. A quarter mile from shore, the skippers at their posts in the conning towers gave orders to reverse engines. As the profiled hulls came to a halt, the rubber rafts plopped over their sides. Two men slid into each boat and started to paddle energetically toward the beach. The U-boats maneuvered to bring their sterns around so they would face open water.

"Let's go." Rednitz started to rip off his shoes.

Hochbauer and Schmidt hesitated.

"Come on. It's no colder than last night."

It was forty-five degrees. Hochbauer and Schmidt unlaced their shoes. Running, they dived into the water.

Gallant watched as the three thrashing figures in the water and one of the rubber boats neared each other. He turned his head skyward, listening.

The two sailors in the raft dropped their paddles and helped the three swimmers heave themselves over the bulky sides. Gallant reached out and took the Sten gun from the man standing alongside him. The sailors picked up their paddles. Their arms were clearly visible in the moonlight as they raised them to thrust the blades into the water.

The safety clicked as Gallant thumbed it off, breaking the silence on the beach. He raised the weapon, then looked skyward again. The man standing next to him did likewise. Gallant sighted on the slowly moving, laden raft.

"I think I hear it," the man said.

A thin drone came from afar. White surged from under the counters of the two U-boats as their propellers beat madly to get them under way. Frantic yells could be heard from the men on the rafts. Gathering speed, the U-boats pulled away from them.

Its engines roaring, a Sunderland dived in for a low-level attack. It headed for the larger of the two craft, the Type IX, U-841. Both boats turned all their fire power on the slow-moving seaplane. As the Sunderland was about to release its bombs, the U-841 heeled over in a turn under full left rudder. Although not yet up to its full eighteen-knot surface speed, the Type IX craft managed to dart out from under the bombs. They exploded nearby, showering her with water.

A second Sunderland winged in to attack the smaller U-536. The VII-C boat took evasive action under full power as its guns hammered the airplane. Both boats continued running on the surface in conformance with admiralty regulations. A dive would leave them sitting ducks for planes already within striking distance. With their surface-speed maneuverability and armament they were more than a match for the slow-moving planes.

The Sunderlands circled to come in again. An engine on the first plane sputtered and started throwing smoke. The plane went into a glide, heading for the water near the shore. The second Sunderland straightened out for a bombing run. In front of it, running east, the two subs were headed, as far as the

Sunderland could see, on a converging course with the *Camrose* and the *St. Catherine*.

As the Sunderland came in, heading for the U-841, the two U-boats spotted the Canadian warships. Caught between the two enemy forces, the U-boats bowed to the stronger. Since early that year, the boats had been stripped of the cannon on their foredecks and were under orders not to fight it out on the surface with naval units. The order to dive was sounded.

The bridges of both craft were cleared in thirty seconds and their hatches closed for the dive. The plane released its bombs. The U-841 turned. The bombs scored no more than a close hit. The waters closed over both boats as they headed down in a crash dive.

On its electric motor the U-841 burrowed its way under, its crew working at top speed to secure the boat. The first sign of something amiss came from a chief petty officer trying to spin the wheel which would close the diesel exhaust valve. The valve, located at the stern of the boat, would not close. Apparently the near miss had done its damage.

The U-boat was at one hundred fifty feet. To continue the dive without determining the extent of the damage might be fatal.

The U-841 came up. It surfaced to find itself on a collision course with the *Camrose*. Only one of its diesel engines was operating. The cylinders of its second diesel were flooded with water by the open exhaust valve. With its speed severely reduced, the U-841 attempted to swing to port to avoid the corvette coming in on its starboard quarter. The maneuver would place its aft torpedo tubes in firing position.

Aboard the corvette the order was given to ram. Its engines stepped up to their utmost revolutions, the *Camrose* swept in to ride over the stern of the U-841, crushing its hull.

Nearby, the U-536 was proceeding at the maximum speed of

its electric engine, trying to outwit the *St. Catherine,* patrolling above her. For the moment, the propellers of the other vessels would confuse the frigate's listening devices. The St. Lawrence currents did as much for her asdic.

The *St. Catherine* laid down a depth-bomb pattern based on a calculation of the sub's course. A half mile east, the U-536, knowing it was safe, reduced speed to conserve its batteries.

On shore, both Canadians and Germans watched the finale of the battle they had engendered. Under guard, the recaptured U-boat skippers together with the four sailors from the rafts shivered in their wet clothing.

In the moonlight, they could see the *Camrose* turning tightly to rush back to the U-841. As she came alongside the sinking hulk, her searchlights were turned on to help pick up the survivors, who could be seen dotting the calm waters.

"How is it in prison camp, sir?" one of the sailors asked Schmidt.

"You'll see," Schmidt replied.

Gallant handed the Sten gun to the man from whom he had borrowed it.

"Well, the war's over for them," the man said.

You'll see ran mockingly through Gallant's head.

THIS BOOK WAS SET IN

CALEDONIA AND GOTHIC OUTLINE TYPES,

PRINTED AND BOUND BY

H. WOLFF BOOK MANUFACTURING CO.

IT WAS DESIGNED BY

LARRY KAMP